Deep Into The Weeds

To Nanette
Enjoy the trip!

WILLIE HANDLER

Black Rose Writing | Texas

©2022 by Willie Handler
All rights reserved. No part of this book may be reproduced, stored in a retrieval system or transmitted in any form or by any means without the prior written permission of the publishers, except by a reviewer who may quote brief passages in a review to be printed in a newspaper, magazine or journal.

The author grants the final approval for this literary material.

First printing

This is a work of fiction. Names, characters, businesses, places, events, and incidents are either the products of the author's imagination or used in a fictitious manner. Any resemblance to actual persons, living or dead, or actual events is purely coincidental.

ISBN: 978-1-68433-946-4
PUBLISHED BY BLACK ROSE WRITING
www.blackrosewriting.com

Printed in the United States of America
Suggested Retail Price (SRP) $19.95

Deep Into the Weeds is printed in Garamond Premier Pro

*As a planet-friendly publisher, Black Rose Writing does its best to eliminate unnecessary waste to reduce paper usage and energy costs, while never compromising the reading experience. As a result, the final word count vs. page count may not meet common expectations.

Other Books by Willie Handler

The Road Ahead

Loved Mars Hated the Food

Deep Into The Weeds

For Jordan and Zachary who

inspire every day.

CHAPTER 1

I lean forward in my seat and look intently across the fake wood-grain desk, staring at Desmond's shifty eyes. The sniveling little bastard shuffles some papers and avoids my gaze. What a dick. I've known Desmond Lamont since we were in high school. He was a bit of dick then too.

His ridiculous moustache—a cross between a caterpillar and toothbrush bristles—is twitching. It looks like it's trying to crawl off his face. His lame combover doesn't quite cover his sweaty balding scalp. The buttons on his white dress shirt strain to contain his oversized gut.

Behind him on the wall is a bank calendar displaying the month of April. The photo for the month portrays a happy family walking in a park. It must have been taken before the friggin' bank cut off their credit.

"Mister McPherson, thank you for coming in today."

Shit. This can't be good.

"Come on, Desmond, we've known each other for over thirty years," I say. "What's with this Mister McPherson bullshit? Get to the point."

Desmond flips through the papers on his desk as if looking for something. "Preston, your application to increase your line of credit has been denied by the bank."

I give him my best gloomy look. My shoulders droop, and my arms fall to my sides. "You must be joking."

"Sorry, I wish I was."

"I don't get it," I blurt out, slumping back into my chair. "I'm selling all the milk we produce. Besides, the farm is worth considerably more than our line of credit. The bank is covered."

Desmond removes his glasses and uses a tissue to clean them, although they aren't dirty. "These decisions aren't made here in the branch. Head office made the call. I'm always fighting for local business folks. Don't make me out to be the bad guy here."

He doesn't fool me. I know he passed the decision up the line to avoid making it himself. He could have backed me up, but he didn't want to stick his neck out. Another knife in the back of dairy farmers in this country.

I'm over the disappointment stage and quickly move to the pissed off stage. "Why was it turned down, then?"

"Our business analysts devalued your farm assets as a result of the U.S. – Canada Dairy Agreement."

I can't believe they're putting so much importance on the new dairy agreement. Sure, prices are falling because of cheaper products from the States, but that's hardly a reason to screw farmers. I feel my face flush as I lean forward, pointing an accusatory finger at him. "That's a bunch of bullshit!"

Desmond flinches at my reaction. "Preston, you know it's true," he says, pulling his glasses off for another cleaning. "Milk prices are dropping, and with it your profit margin and cash flow. That reduces the value of your farm property and your ability to make loan payments."

The muscles in my flushed face tighten. "You know when the farmers in Norfolk County are gone, the town of Delhi and this bank branch are dead, along with it your political career."

Desmond Lamont walks around town with a swelled head. He's not only the manager of the Dominion Bank of Canada branch but also two-term mayor of Norfolk County, which includes Delhi. The town of about seven thousand people in southwestern Ontario is north of Lake Erie. He and his wife, Lucille, are active at our church and the county's annual fall fair. The Lamont's have their fingers in almost everything that goes on in town.

"Preston, why don't you speak to some of the local credit unions. Maybe they can help you."

Go ahead, Dickhead, pass the buck. He knows that they are going to be flooded with loan applications.

"Don't forget, agriculture is the backbone of this country," I say with as much dignity as I can muster. "Farmers put up with random weather, pestilence, and pollution to protect our land and ensure that Canadians have fresh, safe, and healthy produce to eat. We have been the economic engine of this country since before Confederation."

"Preston, that's a lovely speech, but I've heard it before," says Desmond, shifting in his seat. He picks up a pen, clicking the tip up and down. I want to rip it out of his hand. "I've known you and your family for a long time. I fought with our head office folks to try to make this happen. That's not even the worst part."

"What do you mean?" I say, glaring across the desk.

Desmond rises from his chair and stares out the window onto Main Street while pulling on his necktie. No doubt he's trying to put some distance between us. The little prick is probably worried I'll take a swing at him. "You should know that the bank may also call in your line of credit. The decision will come down to things like loan-to-value ratio and cash flow."

"You can't be serious!" I roar, shoving his desk forward. "I'll lose my farm. McPhersons have owned the farm for over one hundred years."

"I'm sorry -"

I leap to my feet and storm out of his office, slamming the door behind me. The noise startles one of the tellers. Oh wait, excuse me, *customer service representatives*. She skitters past me to see if Desmond is still alive.

I step outside the bank and walk past my Chevrolet Cargo truck. I'm too pissed to get behind the wheel. Squinting into the bright sunlight, I check for traffic before crossing Main Street and heading straight to Johnny's Lounge. After stepping inside, it takes my eyes a minute to adjust to the bar's low lighting. The place has a musty sour smell, which most likely originates from all the beer spilt onto the threadbare green carpet. The scarred wood-paneled walls are covered with sponsorship plaques from kids' hockey, baseball, and soccer teams.

It's early afternoon and only a small number of tables are occupied. I walk up to the bar and plop down on a stool. The bar's laminate surface is faded and worn. There's a partially drunk glass of beer next to me in front of an empty seat. On a TV screen over the bar, a sports talk show is playing. The analysts dissect last night's playoff game between the Maple Leafs and Bruins. Someone saunters out of the washroom and sits next to me.

"Mac, what are you doing here at this hour?"

I swing around on my stool and stare at my brother-in-law in uniform. "I should be asking you the same thing, Sergeant Becker," I say, frowning. "Ain't you on duty?"

"I'm on lunch break," he says, smirking.

"Tuck in your shirt, man. You look like a slob."

Fergus Becker is a member of the Norfolk County Ontario Provincial Police Detachment and runs their Delhi satellite office. We're too small to have our own police force, so the OPP assigns twenty cops to the county. Ferg joined the McPherson clan by marrying my sister, Jeannie.

"I didn't see your squad car out front."

"Tyler is doing a brake job," says Ferg, wrapping his pudgy fingers around his glass and draining what was left of his beer. "So, I walked over here for lunch." Ferg will never be on a police recruitment poster. His physique is better suited for a pizza restaurant ad.

"Wow, that's a whole block and a half," I say, holding back a laugh. "That's helluva lot of exercise for you."

"Fuck you, Mac! Look who's talking."

"So, I have some gray hair and wrinkles. Farming is physical labor. I'm in perfectly good shape for a fifty-three-year-old."

"Uh huh," says Ferg with a mocking tone.

I gaze at Ferg's empty glass. "Looks like you came for a liquid lunch."

A bartender I've never seen before walks over to me. He looks barely old enough to drink. His light brown hair is long and tousled. An underachieving scraggly beard covers his cheeks and chin. "Can I get you something to drink?" he asks.

"Yeah, I'll have me a beer."

"We're featuring some local craft beers this month. There's a Salted Brownie Oatmeal Stout and Blueberry Blonde."

Ferg snorts into his empty glass. "Sounds like they belong on your dessert menu. I came in for a beer not lunch. Just bring me a Molson."

"A Molson it is." The bartender grabs an empty glass from a shelf behind him and disappears with it.

"Did you just come from the bank?" asks Ferg.

"Yup."

"I can't believe you dressed in your Sunday church clothes for Dipshit Des. What did he say?"

"The Dominion won't give us any more credit," I spit out. "Not only that, but they could also call in our loan. It seems our dairy business ain't profitable enough for the bank."

The bartender puts down the glass, filled to the brim, on a coaster in front of me. I pick up the glass and drain half of its content, wiping away the remnants of the beer head from my mouth with my sleeve.

"They can't do that," protests Ferg.

"They sure as shit can."

"I'm gonna fix that turd."

"Is that so? How ya gonna to do that?"

"Next time he's out for dinner with Lucille, I'm going to pull him over and ask him to take a breathalyzer," he says with a wink. "I got one rigged that always reads above point zero-eight."

I laugh at the mischievous look on his face. "Ferg, you can't be pulling shit like that. Yer gonna get caught one day."

"The hell I will," he says, pulling his stool closer. "So, what are you going to do if the bank calls in your loan?"

I stare into my near empty glass. "Don't know yet." Thank God my dad isn't around to have to deal with this. This farm has been in the family since 1912 and I'm not ready to give up on it. It's more than just a farm; it's our legacy. I wish the rest of the family would see it that way. "People have lost sight of the fact that agriculture is the backbone of this country. Farmers put up with random weather, pestilence, and pollution to protect our land and ensure that Canadians have fresh, safe, and healthy produce to eat. We have been the economic engine -"

"Mac, save the speech for someone who hasn't heard it yet," Ferg says, rolling his eyes. "Though I doubt you'll find anyone in Norfolk who hasn't be subjected to it."

"Well maybe a lot of folks need reminding."

"How about turning the farm into something more profitable? You got all that land."

"That takes money, too," I say, sighing. "I haven't sat down to look at my options yet, but the Dairy Board is holding an update meeting on the new dairy agreement in Simcoe tonight. I thought I'd drop by and see what bullshit they got to say. You never know. Maybe these clowns have a plan to keep us afloat."

"Keep me in the loop," he says. "I think Tyler should be finished with my cruiser by now. I need to get back to protecting the world from crime and corruption."

Ferg gets up from his stool and drops some change next to his empty glass. "You know we're here to help you and Meryl any way we can," he adds, putting a hand on my shoulder. "We're family."

"Thanks."

I down what's left in my glass and signal the kid behind the bar to bring me another.

***

Walking out of Johnny's, the sunlight reflects off what remains from last night's snow on the rooftops, blinding me momentarily. A crowd of teens is hanging out in front of Subway, but other than that, the slushy sidewalks are almost empty. Once I reach my truck, I yank open the door and nudge myself behind the wheel. The engine roars to life as I turn the ignition. I shift into drive and pull into traffic.

The truck crawls down Main Street until it reaches the edge of town where I turn onto Concession Road #4. On the open road, I gun it, and within minutes pull into the dirt entrance way of McPherson's Dairy Farm. As the truck rumbles toward the farmhouse, I notice the open fields are still partially covered with the remnants of a long winter of snow. The sun has melted enough of the snow so that much of the land is now showing dark stretches of topsoil.

As I step out of the cab of the truck, a gun blast echoes across the property, causing me to flinch. A frightened cow skitters past my truck. I turn to spot a familiar gray-haired woman wearing a coat over a nightgown standing on the porch of the house with a shotgun aimed at me. She takes a few steps forward with a finger still on the trigger.

"Damn it, you could have killed me," I call out. "Mum, what are you doing firing the gun? You scared the shit out of Bess."

"Who's there?" she says, squinting in my direction.

"It's Preston," I say, walking towards her. "Where are your glasses?" Fortunately, she couldn't hit a bull elephant from three feet away without them.

She lowers the shotgun, still squinting. "Thank goodness it's you, son. I thought we were being robbed."

"Mum, why are you in your nightgown? It's the middle of the afternoon."

"Don't be playing no tricks on me. I know it's barely dawn."

I take the gun out of her hands and put the safety lock on while leading her inside. "Where's Meryl?"

"Who?"

"My wife."

"I thought her name is Sally. Why does she keep changing her name?"

I escort Mum to her bedroom. In the hallway, she stops in front of several framed photos of my grandparents. "They hardly ever come around anymore," she says with a sigh.

Once I've safely sequestered Mum inside her bedroom, I pull some clothes out of the dresser and closet. "Get changed while I check to see that Bess is alright."

"Bess? You just said your wife was Meryl."

I shake my head but don't bother to respond. I keep the gun cabinet in my office, and I head back there, moving a stack of papers on my desk so I can put down the shotgun. Pulling open the cabinet doors, it's obvious the last person hadn't bothered to lock it. I carefully place the shotgun in the rack and close the cabinet. I give the combination lock a couple of spins to lock it.

On my way to my bedroom, I pass by Mum's room. I can hear her singing "*Waltzing Matilda*." Poor Mum hasn't been the same since Dad passed away, although she seems to be happy enough. She's become obsessed with TV soap operas.

My denim overalls are stretched out on a chair just as I'd left them earlier in the day. As I strip off my suit, I glance at myself in the dresser mirror. What a sight I am in a jacket and tie. I grab a hanger, place my clothes on it, and put them back in the closet until the next time we go to church.

Stepping outside onto the porch, I stop and gaze across the barren cornfield next to the house. Bess is immediately beyond a ridge, a safe distance from the house. I look down at my feet and realize that I still have my city shoes on. After slipping out of my shoes and pulling on a pair of rubber boots, I slog across the muddy field until I reach Bess.

She looks at me with her deep brown eyes, her nostrils sucking in air. I gently pat her shoulder, and she responds with a soft *moo*. "There, there, girl. Everything is fine. You can come back home."

Bess is the family pet. She was born on the farm but was never a good milk producer. Once cows become poor milkers, they are sold off to a meat processor. But we became attached to Bess and didn't have the heart to sell her off. So, she hangs out at the house. In the summer, to escape the heat, she will wander into the barn with the other cows.

"*Mooooo,*" responds Bess, nodding her head. She turns around and plods back to the house. I fall in behind her. "Bess, how the hell am I gonna save this darn farm? We're being screwed by the bank. I hope the Dairy Board can throw us smaller producers a lifeline."

"*Mooooo.*"

"You're right. They are pretty much useless."

CHAPTER 2

It's a twenty-minute drive to Simcoe, the largest town in the county and about three times the size of Delhi. I stroll into the Norfolk Room in the Simcoe Recreational Center shortly before eight o'clock and find a seat near the back of the hall. The harsh lighting, flat white walls, and dingy gray stacking chairs give the room a dreary look. Still, this facility is better than anything we have in Delhi.

The meeting has been organized by the Dairy Farmers of Ontario, which is responsible for milk marketing in the province. For over fifty years, they've had our backs. By setting the dairy product prices paid by producers, the board has ensured that farmers can make a decent profit. But I'm not sure they can save us this time around.

Gazing around the room, I nod to several familiar farmers sitting close by. There are over one hundred dairy farms in the county and many of the operators are present. The crowd is dressed mostly in denim and flannel and is larger than what usually shows for local board meetings. Some people I don't recognize, but the same grim expression is pasted on every face. The U.S.-Canada Dairy Agreement has upset a lot of folks. Another local farmer, Colin Trent, plops down in the seat in front of me. Colin is a large man with a ruddy complexion and graying five o'clock shadow.

"How's it goin', eh?"

"Evening, Colin."

"Government's really fucked us this time."

"Yup."

"I hear old man Hennessey has his farm up for sale."

"No kidding. He ain't going be the only one."

"What are ya thinking of doing?"

"Don't know yet," I say. "That's why I'm here. Want to see what the board is going to do for us."

"Sweet fuck all," says Colin, snarling. "Nothing they can do."

A voice booms through the speaker system. "Folks, please take your seats; we're ready to start the meeting." Standing at the podium in the front of the room is Greg Stolen, President of the Dairy Board. His family are dairy farmers, but these days he mostly works as an administrator and lobbyist for the dairy community. The room goes quiet and those still standing find somewhere to sit.

"Thank you for coming out tonight," says Greg, leaning forward until he is almost touching the microphone attached to the podium. The sound system distorts his voice, which echoes off the concrete walls. "We are holding similar meetings across the province to explain the U.S.-Canada Dairy Agreement and the board's strategy in responding to it. I want to go over the significant points of the agreement reached last week between our government and the Americans -"

"This is what you arseholes get for voting for that douchebag, Brock, the worst prime minister ever!" someone shouts.

"Come on, guys," pleads Greg, wiping his brow with a handkerchief. "Let's try to keep the meeting constructive. We are still an important sector in the Canadian economy. There are nearly a quarter million people working in the dairy sector, which contributes twenty billion dollars to Canada's gross domestic product. And we need to keep reminding everyone out there."

Greg picks up a remote control from the podium and turns on an audiovisual projector that displays a presentation on a large screen behind him. He runs through all the categories of milk products that have been impacted by the agreement. There's nothing new in his presentation; it's all been reported in the news. The Canadian government caved under pressure from the Americans to provide access to the Canadian markets for U.S. farmers. In exchange, Canada got better access to lumber markets in the U.S. Except the government had always said that the Canadian dairy market was untouchable. The price paid to dairy farmers has already dropped because of cheap American imports.

When the presentation covers how much prices are expected to fall because of American imports, grumbling spreads through the room. At the end of the presentation, Greg opens the meeting up for questions. A line of audience members quickly forms behind the microphone stand in the middle aisle.

The first question comes from an Aylmer farmer I'm familiar with. He's a young guy who took over running his uncle's farm a couple of years ago. None of the old man's kids were interested in farming. "My name's Tyler Staggs. I hear talk that the feds will be providing subsidies to us farmers to compensate for what we're going to lose. What does the Dairy Board know about this?"

"Thanks for coming out tonight, Tyler," says Greg, gripping the sides of the podium. "I've been in constant contact with the federal Minister of Agriculture. The minister is aware of the impact of the agreement and has agreed to provide subsidies totaling 786 million dollars over the next five years. I've pointed out to him that this isn't nearly enough cash, but he says that's all the government will be able to provide. We've also approached his provincial counterpart to see what help the Ontario government is willing to provide, but so far there hasn't been any commitment."

Someone shouts, "The politicians have sold us out!"

Greg turns his head toward the direction of the outburst. "Len, if you got something to say then get up and wait your turn at the mic."

"There ain't nothin' to say," Len grumbles, folding his arms across his chest.

Greg turns back to the lineup in front of the microphone and nods at the next person, an old-timer from outside of London with a huge farm including a herd of over one thousand. "Lloyd Schomberg. Begging for handouts from the government is only going to get us so far," he says. "Can you be more specific on what the milk board is gonna do to help us farmers?"

Greg takes a deep breath and blows it out. "Thanks for the question, Lloyd. We plan to boost our marketing expenditures for the next year. Soon there's going to be American dairy products sitting next to ours on grocery shelves. We are designing a campaign to ask consumers to support Canadian farmers by buying locally produced milk, butter, and cheese. We've test marketed our proposed campaign and consumer response has been incredibly positive. We've also developed a 'locally produced' logo, which we are going to encourage processors to include on their labels, packaging, and containers."

I can't believe it. A friggin' logo. Is that the best they can come up with?

Colin leans back and whispers, "It's like tossing a breath mint at a starving man."

I nod my head. "Pretty much."

Fuck it. I've heard enough. The government has abandoned us. The bank has screwed me. Now the Dairy Board has thrown in the towel. All I got left is the family to keep me afloat.

I get up and walk out into the chilly spring evening to my car.

CHAPTER 3

The next morning, I crawl out of bed at the usual time and get dressed. I grab my travel coffee mug, slip on my rubber boots, and step outside to a raw early morning. The cold wind makes me shiver, and I pull on my collar to keep the chill out. It's almost four-thirty, well before dawn, about the time for the first of three milkings that takes place each day. I climb onto my John Deere tractor that we've owned for decades. I scrounge for spare parts to keep it running. It's one of many things that I do to keep my operating costs manageable. The engine whines for several seconds before roaring to life. I shift into drive, and the tractor lurches forward and rumbles toward the milking barn. The barn lights break up the pre-dawn black. The others have already started bringing in the cows.

I park the tractor near the entrance and shut off the engine. Climbing down from the seat, I grab my mug and stroll into the barn, shutting the door to keep out the gusting wind. Jake is applying iodine to the udders of a cow to sanitize them before connecting the cow to the milking machine. Jake has been with us for eight years. He started working on the farm at seventeen after dropping out of school. Jake isn't the swiftest steed in the herd. In fact, I'm quite sure most of the cows are smarter. But it doesn't take a rocket scientist to hook up a cow to a milking machine and he's been a loyal and reliable worker.

"Mornin', Jake."

Jake looks up. "Hey, Mr. McPherson."

"Any of the cows giving you a hard time this morning?"

He stares ahead for a moment before responding. "Umm, no sir. They never give me any trouble."

"That's good," I say. "You let me know if any of them do."

"I will, Mr. McPherson."

"How are the two calves that were born Tuesday doing?" I ask, grabbing a pair of rubber gloves out of a box on the shelf and shoving my hands into them.

"One of 'em looks sad to me," says Jake, frowning.

"Is that so," I say. "Better let the vet know, so he can have a look at them when he comes in."

At the far end of the barn, my daughter Sara leads a group of cows into separated stalls where the milking takes place. She waves when she spots me. The three of us are all that's needed to get the milking done. Less than half of the herd of 440 cows are producing milk at any given time. The rest are too young to impregnate. Like humans, cows produce milk only after giving birth. To continue producing milk, each cow needs to have at least one calf each year.

Sara walks toward me. "How did last night go?"

"A total waste of time. All they're prepared to do is launch some consumer advertising and call it a day."

"That's too bad," she says, while kicking some mud off her boots. "Are we going to be alright? It sounds like we could lose the farm."

"Don't worry," I say, grabbing a bottle of iodine. "I'm calling a family meeting this week. We need to discuss our options."

"Got any good ideas?"

"Nope, but we'll need to come up with some," I say, while bending down to hook up a cow.

We work in silence for the next hour or so except for the occasional *moo* coming from a cow. When the entire herd has been milked, I park myself in front of the computer in the staff room. Sara slips in and stands behind me, looking at the screen. "How many cows are ready to be inseminated?"

"I'll print off the list for you," I say. "We may need to order more *stud juice* though."

"I'll check the bull semen inventory."

"Look at this," I say, pointing at the monitor. "We have some drop off in milk production from a few cows that are still young. They've been like that for over a week."

"Hmm, when the vet drops in, I'll have him check them out."

My phone chirps "Ask Me How I Know" by Garth Brooks. I fish the phone out of my pocket. It's one of the farm hands, John. "Mornin'. How's our heifer doing?"

"It's been over an hour and she's stopped pushing."

"Gotcha. I'll be right over."

I shove the phone back into my pocket. "Looks like the heifer in labor will need help."

"Do you need an extra set of hands?" asks Sara.

"No, I should be fine. I'll take a quick peek. If it's a complicated delivery, I'll get the vet here right away. Otherwise, I can do it on my own."

I print off the lists for Sara and shut down the computer. I lumber outside with my empty mug to the tractor. I have this sinking feeling this will all come to end soon. Raising dairy cows is the only life I've ever known. What else would I do?

CHAPTER 4

It's after dinner later in the week, and the family squeezes around our dining room table. Mum bought the Colonial dining room set back in the seventies. Over the years, hundreds of family dinners and meetings have taken place in this room. Every nick and crevice in the table has a story to tell. Over that time, Dad passed away, our daughter Sara has moved out, and so much more.

At the end of the table is Ferg, telling an off-color joke to Uncle Liam. Liam is Dad's brother, and the two of them ran the farm until my father passed away eleven years ago. I ran the farm with my uncle for another two years, and then Aunt Marie died. At that point, Liam said he was done with farm life and handed over the operations to me.

Liam's son, and my cousin Graham, is standing in the corner, ignoring everyone while focused on his phone. He's a lawyer in Toronto and couldn't care less about the farm. He considers it an asset and would love to see it sold off. His wife never comes out to the farm. She's too busy chauffeuring around their two overindulged children from one program to another.

Mum slinks into the dining room, wearing the gown she had bought for a family wedding. "How lovely of you all to come for our wedding anniversary."

Meryl returns from the kitchen carrying a large tray with a silver tea set on it. When she sees Mum, she abandons the tray on the table. "Come on, Mum," she says, grabbing Mum's hand. "Let's get you into something more comfortable."

"Good idea," says Mum. "This is an awfully dull affair."

When Meryl returns and everyone settles around the table again, I begin the meeting. "Thanks for coming out tonight. I'm going to get right to the point.

McPherson's Dairy Farm is at a crossroads. The environment around us is changing and we need to change with it."

"If we're here so you can tell us that you're planning to make changes here," says Uncle Liam, "Let me remind you that I still own half the farm."

I throw my arms up in the air. "Just relax. Decisions regarding the farm have always been made by all family members. That's not going to change."

"Mac, we all know about the dairy agreement," interjects Graham. "So, I assume the farm is no longer profitable."

"Not necessarily," says Meryl, walking around the table with the tea pot refilling cups. "I've been going over the books and doing some number crunching. We can maintain profits even if milk prices drop further by reducing our labor costs."

"How is that possible?" asks Uncle Liam. "Are you people gonna give up sleeping?"

"By buying robotic milking machines," says Sara. I had filled her in on my idea shortly before the meeting and she was totally on board.

"That's right," I say. "We've worked it out, and if we expand our herd slightly, we can justify picking up three robot milkers. We will be able to get rid of most of our part-time employees."

"How much will the machine costs?" asks Graham.

"About three-quarter of a million."

"Wow! That much?" responds Graham. "But if you can pull it off, I think the family is cool with the plan." He looks over at his father. "Right, Dad?"

"I agree," adds Liam. "Provided that you can still make some money."

"There is one catch," I say, shifting my eyes around the room. "It seems the bank isn't as supportive. They've cut off our line of credit. That's one of the reasons I called this meeting. We are hoping the family can help us out."

"Look, Preston, the bank is obviously trying to tell you something," says Graham, rapping his index finger on the table. "I agree that we've reached a crossroad. But the right road to follow involves selling the farm. I estimate that we'll all walk away with enough money to live comfortably for years to come."

"We can't sell the family farm," responds Sara, her eyes welling up. "Isn't that right, Mum?"

Mum's back stiffens, and her head jerks up at the mention of her name. "Over my dead body! They can throw me in jail."

"No one is going to jail, Mum," I say, looking down the table at the stone faces. "Remember that agriculture is the backbone of this country. Farmers put up with random weather, pestilence, and pollution to protect our land and ensure that Canadians have fresh, safe, and healthy produce to eat. We have been the economic engine of this country since before Confederation."

"Oh, God, it's the farming speech again," says Graham, rolling his eyes.

"At least think about it. I'm willing to pay a competitive rate of interest to those willing to lend us funds."

"Count me out," says Liam, slapping his palm on the table. "I don't like the prospect of having to foreclose on my own nephew."

"Well, if you can't make a living under the current conditions and you can't afford to modernize the farm," says Graham, picking at a slice of Meryl's apple pie, "I don't see any other options available to you."

"I do," says Ferg. Everyone looks at the end of the table. Ferg has been quiet up to now, which is not his nature. He's always in the middle of every conversation. "You could always convert the farm to something more profitable."

"Like what?" I ask.

"How about marijuana?"

"We're having a serous conversation," says Meryl.

"Ferg, this isn't a good time for one of your lame ideas," I say.

"I'm being serious," says Ferg as he reaches across the table to grab two cookies off a platter. "Since the government has legalized the stuff, it's been flying off the shelves. There's good money to be made here."

"I don't know the first thing about growing marijuana," I say.

"I'm with Mac on this one," says Graham, frowning at Ferg. "The prudent thing to do would be to sell this place and live off the investment interest."

"Dad, you should think about it," implores Sara. "Besides, pot has to be the one of easiest crops to grow."

"You realize it's going to cost money to convert the farm from livestock to crop," I say, stroking the stubble on my chin. "That's the point of this meeting. We can't get any more credit from the bank."

"You may not need to borrow money to set up a weed farm," says Ferg, cookie crumbs flying out his mouth. "I know a guy who can provide the seed money for a share of the revenue."

I look over at him with pursed lips. "Jesus Murphy. How would you know anyone with deep pockets?"

"It just so happens that in the past year, the OPP brought in a consultant to do some training on cannabis legalization. I got to talking to one of the company executives, and he told me that they provide a lot of different types of services including setting up and investing in farms."

"What's the name of this so-called consultant?" asks Meryl, eyeing him with a wrinkled brow.

"Jimmy Scarpini."

Ferg and I are like brothers, but he can come up with some of the dumbest shit. "This sounds like another one of your half-baked schemes," I say. "Like the time you wanted to sell fake stick-on car sunroofs."

"Hey, I still think they were cool looking," says Ferg. "Who knew they would peel off in the sun? As for Jimmy, he's totally legit. The OPP isn't going to bring in mobsters for training. Come on, Mac. It doesn't hurt to at least talk to him."

"Look I'm not interested," I reply with a stoic expression locked on my face. "Does anyone have any other ideas? Something that doesn't involve the drug trade."

"Go ahead and look for your savior," says Graham, smirking. "Meanwhile, I'll start checking out brokers for when you're ready to sell."

CHAPTER 5

I kneel behind the tractor to lock in the trailer hitch. The wind makes my eyes tear and I straighten up to wipe them with my sleeve. I look over my shoulder at the trailer filled with cow manure. Each day, I take all the manure scraped off the barn floors by our automated collection system and drive it to a collection pool. The manure is made into fertilizer, which we use on the feed corn grown in the fields. The smell of manure is everywhere, but when you've lived your entire life on a farm, you don't even notice.

I hold a grab bar at the side of the tractor with my left hand, step onto the foot platform, and pull myself into the driver's seat. As I start the engine, another tractor rumbles toward me with Jake behind the wheel. I shift the tractor into gear and meet him part way.

"Hey, Mr. McPherson. There's a feller at the house looking for you."

"Thanks, Jake. I am expecting him but not this early," I say, climbing down from the tractor. "Why don't you take this tractor and drop off the manure for me?"

"Sure thing, Mr. McPherson," he says as he hops to the ground.

We swap vehicles and I turn the other tractor around, riding it toward the house. I pull my collar tightly around my neck to stay warm, shielding myself from the wind that whips across the open fields. As I reach the crest of the gravel road, I see a black S-Class Mercedes parked out front of the house. This guy has deep pockets and isn't embarrassed about letting people know. Right in front of the car is Bess, eyeing the visitor suspiciously.

When I pull up behind the car, a tall heavy-set man gets out. This snot is barely in his thirties. How the heck did he get this successful at his age? *Look at Mr. Fancy*

Pants. He's wearing a black wool coat over a dark business suit and black oxford shoes. Not your typical farm gear. On the right side of his neck is a tattoo partially exposed. It's either a snake or dragon. His hair is thick and swept back with a high bald fade on the sides. It looks like it's been dyed blond. *He looks like he's never gotten his hands dirty but he's going to tell me about farming.*

He walks over with his hand reaching out to greet me. "Hey, I'm Jimmy Scarpini. You must be Preston."

I wipe my hand on my pants and grip his hand. "Yeah, I know who you are. You're the feller who thinks he's going to tell me all I need to know about farming."

Jimmy is nervously gazing at Bess from the corner of his eye. "What's with the cow? Should he be here?"

"First thing, that cow is a *she*," I say, trying to hold back a laugh. "You can tell the difference between a cow and bull by looking at their undercarriage. Bess is a family pet and likes to hang out at the house."

"She better not do anything to my car," he says, still eyeing Bess.

"She won't, unless the car does something to her first."

"So, Sergeant Becker tells me you are interested in growing cannabis on your farm."

"I'm gonna be straight with ya," I say, still studying the townie in front of me. "I'm not interested in growing cannabis or whatever you call it these days. This is a dairy farm and I'm determined to keep it that way. My pain-in-the-ass brother-in-law has been calling and texting me every day for over a week to meet with you. I'm only doing this to get him off my back."

"I get it. If you want me to leave, that's fine. I can tell him we met and leave it at that."

"You're already here so I might as well give you my standard guided tour and you can tell me about your company."

"That sounds fair. Once I look around," says Jimmy, "it'll give me an idea of what needs to be done to get you prepped for growing in case you change your mind."

"Like I said, I ain't growing nothing here but cow feed."

"Of course, Preston. There'll be no hard sell from me. Where should we start?"

I look down at his feet "Let's start with your shoes. Wouldn't want those Gucci's to get covered in manure."

I step onto the porch and pull out a pair of booties from a box. "I keep these around for visitors. Put them on."

"Thanks," says Jimmy as he bends over to pull the booties over his shoes.

"I'll spare you a tractor ride," I say, directing him to the Ford Explorer parked in front of the garage. "We can drive around in this."

My car chirps as I unlock the doors. I swing open my door and slide behind the wheel. Jimmy gets into the passenger seat, straightening out his fancy coat so it doesn't wrinkle. I grin; such a city slicker. I crawl up the road towards the far end of the farm.

"This farm was purchased by my great-grandfather, Angus McPherson, in 1912 shortly after coming to Canada from Scotland. So, I'm the fourth generation to work this land."

"It's great to see family-run farms like this."

"There are two houses on the property. We live in one, and the other is now unoccupied." I say, pointing to a building at the end of the roadway. "My Uncle Liam's family were the last people to live there." I turn off onto a narrow rocky road. "Just over there is the first barn built on the property. It was put up by my great-grandfather. The barn is in such bad shape, it's a wonder that it hasn't fallen over in a windstorm."

Jimmy pulls a pack of cigarettes and a lighter from his coat pocket. "Do you mind if I smoke?"

I partially lower the passenger window. "Go right ahead."

He pulls a cigarette out of the package and holds it between his lips. "Do you want one?"

"Don't smoke," I say.

Jimmy flips open the lighter, holding the flame over the end of the cigarette until it begins to burn. "Aren't there any other family members working on the farm anymore?" he asks as he fills his lungs with smoke and then slowly blows it out.

"My daughter works full-time at the farm but chooses to live in town."

Jimmy holds the cigarette out the open window. "How large is the farm?"

"We've got 350 acres. It's early in the season, so you can't tell yet, but we use more than half of the land to grow corn to feed the cows. That cuts down on our feed costs."

"You've got a big property. More than you would ever need to grow weed. The largest cannabis farm in Canada is probably no more than ten acres."

This guy has a one-track mind. "Except that I ain't goin' to be growing any weed."

When we reach the unoccupied house at the far end of the property, we turn around and rumble toward the barns.

"Look, I'm talking hypothetical here," he replies. He takes another drag from the cigarette and then tosses it out the window. "I'm not telling you what to do. I'm just saying this is a big property and, as a grower, you could even profit by selling a piece of land to a neighbor."

"Look here. I'm not selling any McPherson land," I growl, glaring at him.

"Hey, man. It's cool."

I park close to the entrance of the first barn and turn off the ignition. We both get out of the SUV and slam the doors shut. Jimmy has his hands in his coat pockets, peering into the closest barn. "How come you have so many barns?" he asks.

"They serve different functions," I say as I lead him inside. "This is the milking barn. Three times a day we bring the cows in here and hook them up to milking machines." I grab a set of teat cups to show him.

"They aren't milked by hand?"

"Heck, no. We couldn't possibly milk a herd this size by hand. It takes thirty minutes to hand-milk a cow. One of these contraptions will do it in three minutes."

"They don't mind?"

"They don't got much feeling down there. A vacuum system draws up the milk. Let me show you where the milk is collected."

I lead him through a doorway off the front entrance. Inside is a large storage tank connected to a system of hoses. "The milking machines pump milk into this baby," I say, slapping my hand on the side of the tank. "We test the milk daily, and it's then picked up and delivered to a processor."

"From my perspective, you're better positioned to move into cannabis than you realize," says Jimmy. His body twists around as he scans the dozen hoses that lead into the top of the stainless-steel tank in the middle of the room.

"How ya figure?"

"You're already producing a heavily regulated product and understand how to maintain a highly sterile environment."

"I don't know about that. There's a big difference between managing livestock and crops."

"Excuse me, Mr. McPherson." We both turn toward the door.

"Sorry to bother you," says Jake, standing outside the door with his hands in his pockets. "I wanted to let you know the feed delivery is here."

"Thanks," I say.

Jake lumbers towards Jimmy, displaying a big grin. "I'm Jake."

Jimmy instinctively covers his nose with his hand in response to the strong manure odor that follows Jake around. Jake extends his hand and Jimmy reluctantly accepts it. "Jimmy Scarpini."

Even Jake likely notices how out of place Jimmy looks in a barn. "What kind of business are you in, Mr. Scarpini?" asks Jake.

"I'm involved in cannabis cultivation."

"What's that?" asks Jakes with a look of confusion.

"You know...weed," says Jimmy.

"You mean like dandelions?" asks Jake, scrunching up his face. "Why would ya wanna grow weeds?"

"He's talking about marijuana," I say.

"Holy Jesus!" cries Jake, his eyes bulging and mouth falling open. "Ain't that illegal?"

"Jake, the government legalized marijuana some time ago," I say. "It's now a cash crop like tobacco and soybean."

Jake lets out a whistle. "I never heard about that."

"Mr. McPherson...umm, Preston and I are discussing options on possibly of growing some here," says Jimmy.

"Wait until my folks hear about this," says Jake, a big grin on his face.

"Settle down, son," I say. "I'm not looking to grow no such thing here. Why don't you take care of the feed delivery while I finish up with Jimmy?"

"Gotcha, Mr. McPherson. Nice meeting you, Mr. Scarpini."

Jake continues to stand there with his mouth gaping open. You never quite know what's going through that head of his. Probably most of the time nothing. "Is there something else on your mind?" I ask.

"No, sir."

"Then why are you still here? Don't you have a feed delivery to take care of?"

A red glow spreads across Jake's face. "Umm...it's just that I never seen a drug dealer before."

"Jesus Murphy, he's not a drug dealer. Now get going, and I'll catch up with you shortly."

He scampers out of the barn, almost tripping over a wheelbarrow sitting at the entrance.

"He seems like a nice kid," says Jimmy after Jake leaves.

"Yup, but I sometimes wonder about that boy. Some drink from the fountain of knowledge, but I think Jake must have only gargled."

Jimmy smirks. "I think I know what you mean."

I take Jimmy back outside. "I don't want to bore you. You don't have to see the other barns."

"I don't mind. Your farm kicks ass."

We walk up to the adjacent barn. "Thanks…I think." I turn toward Jimmy and notice his tailored wool coat has mud splattered on it. *Who the fuck wears that to visit a farm?* "This is the main barn."

We step inside a long barn divided into two open sections where cows freely wander around. "You've got quite an operation here," remarks Jimmy, leaning on a barrier. "It's pretty cold in here. Aren't your barns heated?"

"These here girls like the cold," I say, reaching over a barrier to pat the side of a cow. "Our cows are kept indoors year-round in a controlled environment. See those big overhead fans? They keep the cows cool in the hot weather. I'd rather keep my cows inside, especially during the summer. They can get stressed from the heat, which will lower milk production."

"Hey, what are those things?" asks Jimmy, pointing to one of the cow brushes in one of the pens. A cow moves up against one of the cylindrical yellow nylon brushes, which activates the overhead motor, causing the brush to slowly rotate.

"The brushes calm and clean the cows."

"Are you fucking with me?" asks Jimmy, shaking his head. "I've never heard of that."

"Sort of works like rubbing a dog's belly. Happy cows are productive cows."

"I had no clue how involved a dairy farm can be."

"In this barn, we keep all our milk-producing cows. We buy bull semen, which is used to artificially inseminate the cows."

"Umm, don't bother to go into the details," says Jimmy, looking squeamish.

His reaction makes me grin. "When they give birth, the calves are kept separate in hutches for the first two months to protect them from disease. The hutches are right around the corner," I say, pointing in the direction of the back of the barn. "After two months, the heifers are moved to the barn next door."

"What's a heifer?"

"A young female cow that hasn't produced offspring. I think you'd call them virgins. We keep them away from the larger animals, so they won't get intimidated. At eighteen months, they're ready to be inseminated and moved into the main barn."

I lead him outside. "We won't bother going next door. It looks the same as this one."

"Okay, I really appreciate you showing me around," says Jimmy as he reaches into his pocket for another cigarette. "Why don't we head back to your place and chat."

I fling open the driver's door to the Explorer. "Yeah, that's fine. I've got some time before the girls get milked again."

Several minutes later, Jimmy, Meryl, and I are sitting at our kitchen table in front of steaming cups of coffee.

"Meryl and Preston, you have a nice operation here, and I don't blame you for wanting to keep the dairy farm going," says Jimmy, raising the mug to blow on the coffee. "But there's real good money being made on weed. The greenhouses don't take up much space. You could likely manage both at the same time."

"I know," I say, sipping at my coffee. "It's just that I've always seen myself as a dairy farmer. I know that times are changing, and it's getting harder for independent farmers to compete and make a living. Still, I like what I do and love working with the animals."

"I'm also concerned about how the community will react to us growing marijuana," says Meryl. "This is a small community and very conservative."

"Cannabis is the next big wave. You don't want to miss out."

"It's not just about the money," she responds.

"You certainly have more than enough land for a substantial cultivation operation," says Jimmy, pulling apart a homemade scone. "You can do other stuff with the farm. If you chose not to continue dairy farming, you might decide to pull down the barns or -"

"Hang on there," I say, banging on the table so hard the cutlery rattles. "My Daddy and Granddaddy built those barns."

"Hey, I'm only bouncing around ideas."

"Not that I'm considering this, but what would be involved in setting up a cannabis farm?" I ask.

"We would need to construct about five greenhouses and another structure for drying and trimming."

"That's another reason why this won't work. I don't have that kind of money to sink into the farm. I'm already having issues with the bank."

"We can take care of that too. The company I represent, Green Fields, will get you licensed. Then, they will either find investors that will meet the approval of the government, or we might choose to invest directly in your farm, construct the facilities, and buy all the equipment. You run the place and hire what staff you need."

"We don't know the first thing about growing marijuana," says Meryl. "We've never even tried the stuff."

"That's okay. We'll provide training and help you find staff with experience in large scale cannabis operations."

I lean back in my chair, taking this all in. He's a typical salesperson, making it sound so easy. "You ain't going to be doing this out of the goodness of your heart," I say, my face tightening as I press my lips together. "What's your take?"

"Green Fields would expect you to provide an ownership interest in your farm and a share of the profits," he says, looking at me directly in the eyes. "Our CFO would be able to work out the numbers and provide you with an offer."

A voice booms from outside the door. "Offer for what?"

We turn in the direction of the voice and find Mum standing at the door, her arms crossed, and her nostrils flared.

Jimmy gets up and extends his right hand to greet her. "Nice to meet you Mrs. McPherson. I'm Jimmy Scarpini and -"

"I know who you are. You're some kind of flim-flam man, trying to steal our farm," she barks, refusing to shake his hand.

"No, not at all," he says, flashing her a big grin. "We're talking about an investment opportunity."

"If my husband was still alive, he'd fill your ass with buckshot." She reaches for a broom sitting in the corner by the door and takes a big swing, hitting Jimmy in the back.

"Mum, stop that!" I yell, yanking the broom from her hands. "You can't be whacking company."

"I sure as shit can when they are trying to steal our property."

"He's not stealing nothin'. The bank is on the verge of shutting us down and Jimmy is offering to help us." I look over to Jimmy as a flush spreads across my cheeks. "Look, I'm terribly sorry."

Jimmy is rubbing his back. "Don't worry about it. Think about what we talked about. It was a pleasure meeting with you both."

As Jimmy walks out the door to his car, Mum grabs the broom again and runs onto the porch. "Then next time you come by here, I won't be holding no broom. It'll be my shotgun."

After Mum settles down, I corner Meryl who is clearing the coffee mugs from the table. "I've been thinking about getting Mum checked out."

Meryl sighs. "I've had the same thought. She's always acted weird, but she seems to be getting worse."

"Yup. I talked to Dr. Shindle. He's given me the name of a geriatrician in London. I think I'm going to give him a call and set up an appointment for her."

"You know, that's a great idea."

CHAPTER 6

Somehow, word gets out that I'm looking into growing marijuana. By the end of the week, I have twenty-four messages on LinkedIn and Facebook from cannabis company executives, entrepreneurs, opportunists, and God only knows who else. I'm considering my options, and the next thing I know everyone wants to be my best friend and business partner.

I discover this one on LinkedIn one morning:

Hey Preston! We're looking for investment opportunities in the cannabis sector. Call me right away! 886-555-1246.

This message pops up on Facebook on the same day. I immediately delete it.

Bro! Im a entrapranewer. Looking to source a growing weed biz. Paying top $$$. Dude lets make this happen. PM me.

People reach out to me not only on social media but by phone. I have no idea how they got hold of my cellphone number. Some are reasonably polite, but others are way too aggressive. Most are obnoxious yahoos.

I decide maybe it won't hurt to meet some of these other people. It's not that I've necessarily decided to move forward on growing weed; I want to know what other opportunities are open to me. And I admit all the fuss has got me curious.

On the morning of our first day of interviews, I'm wired from too much caffeine while waiting for Meryl to show up from a trip to the grocery store. I check my watch for the one thousandth time. She has booked the people coming in and will be taking notes. I'm fortunate that she is so skilled at bookkeeping and administration because I'm only good at shoveling cow dung.

The sound of tires grinding on gravel catches my attention. I step out onto the porch as our Ford Explorer SUV pulls up to the house. The driver door flings open and out steps Meryl. She's wearing jeans and a black leather bomber jacket that matches her raven shoulder-length hair.

She goes to the back of the vehicle and raises the hatch. "Can you give me a hand with the groceries?" she calls out.

I lumber over to the car, scooping up several bags in each hand. "What time is the first appointment again?"

"Relax, Mac. We have another two hours to go," she says, pressing the button to lower the hatch with a free hand.

At the front door, I kick off my boots and scoot into the kitchen with the bags of groceries. After placing her bags on the gray quartz kitchen countertop, she spots the empty carafe of coffee. "Did you drink the entire pot of coffee?"

"Umm, I might have."

"You are officially cut off."

I empty the contents of a grocery bag and chuck items into the pantry. "So, how is this going to work again?"

Meryl reorganizes everything I've shoved onto the shelves. "I made six one-hour appointments for those that you wanted to give an opportunity to pitch an offer."

We don't even make appointments with everyone who contacts us. I decide to reject people who seem too shady or desperate. "Are we going to be doing back-to-back meetings?"

"Yup. I told you that already."

"Oh, God. Make lots of coffee," I say, picking up the empty carafe to check if there are dregs left in it.

"No more coffee for you!"

Just over an hour later, we are sitting around our dining room table, listening to pitches. Always the obliging hostess, Meryl serves pots of coffee and homemade apple muffins. It's a crazy scene. We have presenters fly in from across the country - British Columbia, Alberta, and Quebec. I feel like a lottery winner, and everyone wants a piece of the prize money.

We don't say much and let the presenters talk. Some bring fancy bound booklets describing their business model. We had PowerPoint presentations complete with animation and fancy graphics. The presentations are all over the map. We get lowball offers to sell the farm. I make it clear that I'm not looking to sell. My favourite pitch is made by Phil from Kelowna. Phil is in his early forties and has been in the "business" for over a decade prior to legalization. He claims that he knows what it takes to run a profitable grow-op.

"Preston, do you realize how much this business will be worth in a couple of years?" I shake my head but say nothing. "After a few years, we could be producing 300 million dollars in product a year and split the profits fifty-fifty."

I may not be an expert on growing weed, but I also didn't just fall off a turnip truck. My faculties are fully functioning. Based on the little research I've already done, that will mean my little farm will become one of the largest growing operations in Canada - maybe the world. At the end of the hour, I thank Phil for flying in all this way to meet with us.

Our meetings go into a second day and then a third day. I have the impression that these slick businesspeople think I'm a country bumpkin, someone who is impressed by the big numbers and ideas that they throw around.

On day two, Blair—who is a venture capitalist from Ottawa—begins his presentation with some words of advice. "Cannabis is a high-tech industry. It's not like raising cattle. Gone are the days where stoners bought some seeds and planted them in their backyard. Growers are using cloud technology, biosynthesis, robotics, programmable lighting, and controlling greenhouse environments using sensors." I don't bother to respond. I'm sure he thinks I sit on a stool while hand milking my cows all day long.

These fast-talking opportunists can't fathom that maybe I'm a competent businessman and entrepreneur. That's what farmers are. Instead, I discover that, in their minds, I'm a commodity. When a presenter talks down at us, Meryl and I avoid making eye contact with each other for fear of breaking out into laughter.

Later that day, we have a mini crisis on our hands. Glen, from Vancouver, and Yvan, from Montreal, show up for the same timeslot. We messed up. Neither is interested in rescheduling and they both take a seat at our dining room table.

I'm still trying to sort out how to deal with these two when Glen launches into his presentation. "I want to discuss the advantages of my company's distribution channels."

"Glen, your company is quickly falling behind," says Yvan. "Our cloud-based sales and distribution network are cutting edge."

Glen is shaking his head. "Technology is just a piece of the puzzle. We are a people-based enterprise with an award-winning call center."

Yvan lets out a laugh. "I hear that you lead the sector in returned products, so you must have a damn busy call center."

"I hear your cutting-edge technology is always crashing."

"Our company is a pioneer in the industry and willing to wager we'll be around a lot longer than yours."

This is how the hour went. Meryl and I sit in silence until I tell them their time is up. Neither one of them got to make their pitch.

On day three, a relatively well-known CEO arrives to make a pitch. I did some research on him and he is worth millions. He's been featured in the Financial Post and Bloomberg, hangs out with music celebrities, and owns three homes. A fancy Piaget watch flashes in the light when we shake hands; it's likely worth more than my car. He uses this folksy approach, which I figure was decided in advance because we're farmers. "You can call me Bud. Is it alright to call you Preston?"

"Mac is fine."

"You have a charming little home," he says, looking around the room and forcing a smile.

"Thank you," responds Meryl.

"And thanks to both of you for finding the time to meet with me," he says through his wide grin. "You folks must be so busy."

I keep from rolling my eyes. "Not a problem. We've set aside a couple of days to speak to people in the industry like you. We have an hour, so the time is all yours."

He hands us swanky bound copies of his presentation, but his preference was to fly us out west to wine and dine us, where he can get us into a boardroom for some high-pressure tactics. Like that's ever going to happen.

It sounded so positive. When his hour is up, I nudge him toward the front door. "Thanks for coming to see us. I'm going to run your proposal by a lawyer and will get back to you."

"No, no, don't do that! We don't need lawyers." *Can you imagine doing a multi-million-dollar deal without a lawyer?* That's when I decide it would be a good idea to get some legal input. Graham has referred me to an experienced cannabis lawyer who looks over the offer. Several days later the lawyer contacts me. "That's a bad deal."

Then there was the real shady guy. How did we know? He never gave us his full name.

"Welcome Mr..." I say as I reach out to shake his hand.

"You can call me Steve."

I get the impression that Steve isn't his real name. Seems more like an "Ice Pick" Paulo type to me.

Meryl offers to take his leather jacket and hang it in the closet, but he refuses. He's wearing a white t-shirt underneath his jacket, ill-fitting black khakis, and red high-top sneakers.

"Do you have a business card?" asks Meryl.

He reaches into his jacket. "Oh, I must have forgotten them."

We take our seats at our dining room table. I look over at Steve, waiting for him to start his pitch, but all we get is awkward silence. He looks at us with a blank look, waiting for us to say something while he gnaws at a piece of gum. Darn it; I hate gum chewers. They remind me of our cows chewing on their cud. "Umm, you have one hour, so the time is all yours."

Steve shifts forward in his seat. "Yeah, yeah. I got a lot of weed experience. Growing, selling, and distribution. I heard you were looking for help and that's why I'm here."

I nod my head. "And how did you hear about us?"

"I never disclose my sources. I'm a discreet businessman."

This is how the meeting proceeds. We finally end it early. Steve creeps us out and we can't wait to get rid of him.

When we finally end the process, I am sure about one thing: I have no desire to do business with any of these people. The cannabis business is too slick and sleezy for plain folks like us. I'm sticking to what I know best.

CHAPTER 7

I stare at the registered letter on the kitchen table. I've read it over three times, but my brain refuses to process the words. *'We regret to inform you that your loan with the Dominion Bank of Canada is being recalled.'*

"Goddammit!"

Meryl pokes her head into the kitchen. "What's wrong?"

"The friggin' bank is recalling our loans. They've given us thirty days. We're done. Toast."

Meryl plops down onto the chair next to me. "We'll just have to find another lender," she says as tears well up in her eyes.

"No one is lending money to dairy farmers these days."

"There must be someone who still does," she says, grabbing my hands in hers.

"Even if there is, we aren't going to find a lender in just a month," I say, pulling away from her as I get up from my seat and grab a jacket.

"Mac, where are you going?"

"To the bank," I answer. "I'm giving Desmond a piece of my mind."

By now, my anger has turned to rage. I race to my truck and push the pedal to the floor. While tearing down Concession Road #4, I hear the high-pitched whoop of a siren. I pull over to the shoulder while looking at my rear-view mirror and lower my window. A familiar figure climbs out of the cruiser and plods toward my truck.

"What the hell is wrong with you?" asks Ferg, poking his head into my truck.

"Fuck off, Ferg," I say with a shaky voice.

"Driving like that will get you killed and possibly someone else," he says.

"The only person dying today is Desmond Lamont."

"Relax. No one is dying today," Ferg replies. "Why don't we have a chat over a coffee? I'll meet you at the Timmies on Main Street. And try to keep your speed to under one hundred."

When I arrive at the Tim Hortons coffee shop, Ferg is already there. He's in line ordering coffee, so I nab a table. He joins me minutes later.

Ferg pulls apart a fritter and shoves a piece into his mouth. He looks down at his uniform and brushes sugar flakes off his shirt. "So, what's eating you?"

I pull the letter from my pocket and toss it across the table. "Go ahead and read this," I say. "Then you can hand me your service revolver."

As he reads the letter, his shoulders slump, and his head drops. "Jeez, I'm sorry, Mac. Maybe it's time to consider one of the offers?"

"I don't want to become a marijuana farmer and definitely not considering giving away part ownership of our farm."

"It seems you don't have many alternatives," says Ferg, stuffing the remainder of the fritter into his mouth. He gives it a few chews before swallowing. "You know, at the end of the month when you can't repay the bank, they'll foreclose and sell the farm for you. This way you can at least hang on to part of the farm. Maybe you can work out a deal, so that instead of buying a share of the property, they give you a mortgage. I think it's time to do some negotiating while you still have time."

"What will folks say when they hear I'm growing weed?" I say, shuffling my feet under the table. "This is a pretty conservative community."

"It's none of anyone's business what you do with your farm," he says, scowling with his fists clenched on the table.

Through the restaurant window, I catch sight of a familiar figure scurrying across the street. I jump out of my seat and run to the door.

"Hey, Lamont!" I yell through the open door. "You were the most despised prick in high school and nothing's changed."

Desmond avoids looking my way and picks up his pace as he trots down the street. People turn their heads to see what the ruckus is about. When he reaches his car, he scoots in and pulls out into traffic.

"I know you can hear me, Desmond Lamont! You coward!" I bellow. "Where are you running to? I know where you live!"

I hear a voice next to me. "Let me take care of him," says Ferg as he jogs out the door and dives into his police cruiser.

I chuckle knowing how Ferg will mess with this guy. Then I realize this can only come back to bite us in the ass. I run to my truck and hop in. Two blocks down the street I find both cars pulled over by the curb and park behind Ferg's cruiser.

Ferg is standing next to Desmond's car speaking to him through an open window. As I approach, I hear Ferg say, "I noticed when you were walking to your car that you were stumbling. Have you been drinking today?"

"Sergeant Becker, are you out of your mind?" asks Desmond. "Have you forgotten I'm the mayor?"

"Is that a yes or a no, Mr. Mayor?" responds Ferg with his sternest look.

I grab Ferg by the arm and pull him away from Desmond's car to the front of the cruiser, so we won't be overheard. "This isn't one of your best ideas," I say.

"What are you talking about? I'm trying to keep our roads safe," he says with a wink as he pulls out a breathalyser from his pocket.

"Des is a total prick, but losing your job isn't going to help me," I say, giving him a shove. "You aren't going to get away with this."

"Why should he get away with putting your farm in jeopardy?"

"Look around. Farmers are getting squeezed everywhere."

"But the banks should be helpin' not hurtin'."

"Just let him go," I say, shaking my head.

"Alright. I'll be right back."

Ferg walks back to Desmond's car, poking his head through the open window. "Since you're a respectable member of the community," he says, "I'm going to give you the benefit of doubt. You have yourself a nice day."

When Ferg gets back to his cruiser, I look down at the asphalt road with my hands in my pockets. "I think I've come to the end of the line."

"What do you mean?"

"Maybe it's finally time to get out of the dairy business. I'm going to call Scarpini."

"Really? That's awesome," he says, giving me a big bear hug. "You aren't going to regret this."

"I better not," I say, still leaning against the police cruiser. "The last thing I want to happen is lose the family farm."

CHAPTER 8

Mum picks up a three-year old magazine sitting on the table in Dr. Gruber's waiting room and flips through the pages. "Preston, I don't know why you dragged me all the way out to London to see some hotshot doctor. I ain't sick."

"Mum, I know you're not sick. I told you already this is just a check up. It's a standard thing once you turn seventy-five."

"I've never heard that before. Sounds like BS to me."

Before I can respond, the doctor pops out of his office. "Hello, I'm Dr. Gruber. You must be Mrs. McPherson and her son, Preston."

I jump to my feet and shake his hand. "Yes, nice to meet you."

He smiles and waves us into his office. I step inside, turning around to ensure Mum joins us. The office barely accommodates his desk and two guest chairs.

After we are all seated, he pulls open a file folder. "Thank you for coming to see me today. Mrs. McPherson, I've already had a conversation over the phone with your son, so I would have some background information. I'm a geriatrician, which is a doctor that specializes in the aging process."

"So, what you're telling me is that I'm old," she says with an icy stare.

"Mrs. McPherson, you are as old as you feel. But to be honest, you begin aging once you reach adulthood. I assess where you are in the continuum."

She leans back in her chair with her arms crossed. "Humph."

"So, how does this work, doctor?" I ask.

"I'm going to ask your mother a series of standard questions which I will use as a baseline. Over time, I will likely repeat the assessment and see if there is any significant change. Any other questions?"

"No," I respond.

"Mrs. McPherson, are you ready to begin?" he asks.

"No, but go ahead anyway."

"Splendid. Can you tell me your birth date?"

"You know a gentleman never asks a woman her age."

"Yes, that's true, but I'm a doctor and this is strictly confidential."

"So, you're telling me that doctors don't need to be well-mannered," she says, snarling.

"Of course, we need to be well-mannered and respectful to our patients. I already know your age."

"So, why are you asking then?"

"It's part of the assessment tool. We ask everyone the same questions."

"Mum, just answer the question and stop giving him a hard time," I say.

"Well, if you insist on prying, I was born on November fourth, 1943," she says, scowling. "But don't be spreading that info around."

"Thank you, Mrs. McPherson, and I won't," he says, glancing down on a sheet of paper in front of him. "What is the year?"

"I just told you - 1943."

"I meant what is the current year?"

She lets out a sigh. "Try to be clear, Dr. Brooder, or we'll be here all day. 2018."

"Thank you," he mutters, returning his gaze to the sheet of paper. "And, by the way, it's Dr. Gruber. Now, do you know what day and month it is?"

"June eleventh."

"And do you know where we are now?"

Mum looks around the room. "Dr. Hoover, it looks to me like we're in your office."

"It's Dr. Gruber," he responds. His smile seems more forced. "I'm going to name three objects and ask that you repeat them: tree, apple, chair."

"Tree, apple, chair."

Dr. Gruber hands Mum a piece of paper that says, 'close your eyes.' "Please read this and do what it says."

"How can I read if I have my eyes closed?"

He shakes his head with a look of exasperation. "No. No. Just read it and do what it says."

"Mum, can you please cooperate?" I beg. "Don't waste the doctor's time."

"He's wasting *our* time," she says as she shuts her eyes. "Are you happy now?"

"Thank you," says the doctor. "Earlier I told you the name of three things. Can you tell me what those were?"

"Well, it seems you may be the one with memory problems," she declares. "Maybe you should have written them down."

"My memory is fine. Do you remember the words?"

Her head is cocked to one side as she sighs. "Tree, apple, chair."

This is how it went for the remainder of the assessment. It was like the two of them were sparring. I couldn't help but feel sympathy for the doctor. And a little embarrassed.

When the assessment was over, Dr. Gruber turns to me. "The questions I asked are part of a standard test to evaluate cognitive impairment."

"What's the verdict, doc?"

"Your mother is not suffering from any cognitive deficit," he says while closing the file on his desk. "But without a doubt, she is eccentric."

"Should she return for another assessment in the future?" I ask as the doctor ushers us out of his office.

"Please don't."

CHAPTER 9

The door chime breaks my concentration, and I look away from my computer monitor. The chimes go off again. Grabbing my coffee, I get up and stroll to the front door. Mum beats me there and is eyeballing the guest.

"And who might this exotic-looking gentleman be?" she asks with a less-than-subtle wink.

"Mum, you've already met Jimmy," I say, reaching around her to extend my hand out.

"I don't forget a face," insists Mum, her hands on her hips. "We definitely haven't met."

"Hey, good to see you," responds Jimmy, grabbing my outstretched hand. "And you too, Mrs. McPherson."

I try to steer Jimmy past Mum. "Remember, you accused him of being a flim-flam man who was trying to steal the farm."

"Preston dear, you have such a vivid imagination. Now why didn't you tell me we were having company?" asks Mum. "I would have freshened up."

"Mum, why don't you see if Meryl needs a hand in the kitchen?"

"Meryl?"

"Yes, your daughter-in-law, Meryl."

She heads to the kitchen shaking her head. "So, this week it's Meryl. You shouldn't be playing pranks on your mother."

I put my mug down on the dining room. "Grab a seat. Can I get you a coffee or something else to drink?"

"No, thanks. I'm fine."

Jimmy parks himself on one side of our dining room table, opening a large briefcase bulging with documents, which he spreads out on the table. "As I mentioned on the phone, I want to go over our offer and property development plan."

"Meryl is our business manager," I say. "She needs to be in on this too."

"Meryl, are you almost done?" I call loud enough so she can hear me in the kitchen.

There's a loud crash coming from the other room. "I'm tied up now. Will be out soon."

"Your mom is quite the character," says Jimmy.

I feel my face flush. "You can say that again. She's always been somewhat quirky."

As I pull up a chair opposite him, Jimmy stops shuffling his papers. "First thing, I want to thank you again for your confidence in Green Fields. I had the impression that you weren't interested in moving forward. But we are happy to get this opportunity to work together."

I stare at the pile of papers in front of Jimmy, rubbing my forehead with my hand. "Let's say changing circumstance has forced my hand." I know I'm going to fucking regret this. Every bone in my body is telling me so.

Meryl finally comes out of the kitchen, her smile not quite masking the frustration in her voice. "Sorry for the delay." She grabs the seat next to me.

"No problem," says Jimmy. "Are we ready to do this?"

I nod my head.

"I have three sets of documents for you to review," explains Jimmy. "The first is an agreement to provide Green Fields Corporation with fifty percent ownership of McPherson's Dairy Farm. We've evaluated your property at $12,700 per acre, which works out to a little over two million." He passes a package of documents to our side of the table. "Those funds can go towards paying off the line of credit at your bank and support your family while we get you set up to grow cannabis."

I lean back in my chair with my arms crossed, shaking my head. "I'd say that's a deal breaker. I'm not about to give up even part ownership of this property. This is a family heirloom."

"Relax, Mac. Is there a way to structure this differently?" asks Meryl. "Perhaps as a mortgage. We would use the property to secure the loan and provide you with a return on investment."

Jimmy retrieves the copies of the agreement and shoves them into his briefcase. "Based on the value of this property, that might actually work. This is not normally how we structure a deal, but I will run it by our management team. If they agree, I will have our legal team draft up new documents."

I lean back forward in my seat. That was a slick attempt to pry this farm out of my hands. Are these people any better than the other swindlers who pitched us?

Jimmy holds up another set of documents. "We will assist in building the necessary facilities, purchase equipment, and get you licensed with the feds. All of the details are here."

"So, what's the last package?" I ask.

"I was just getting to that. This is a contract between you and Green Fields. Standard stuff about responsibilities and such."

"Anything we should pay attention to?" asks Meryl as she shuffles through the stack of papers.

"It's all important. Things like how you can only sell your cannabis to Green Fields and, if you ever decide to sell the farm, you have to offer it to Green Fields first. You need to go through all of it."

"I can only sell to you guys?" I ask.

"Who else would you sell to? Drug dealers?"

"Of course not."

"Don't forget that we're providing you with everything – money, plants, technology, training. It's only fair."

"Well, it's also got to be at a fair price," I respond. "I ain't born yesterday. I don't want to be like a pizza chain franchise owner - slave labor for some corporation."

"You will always be treated fairly."

The stack of paper in front of us grows. What have I got us into? It looks like another bill from the cannabis lawyer.

"Umm, there's one other thing." I say, clearing my throat. "The bank plans to start foreclosure on us in eleven days. How soon can we get a decision regarding the mortgage?"

"You will hear from me in the next couple of days. I can set up a time next week to execute these agreements if you're ready to do so. I'll have a bank draft cut for you. Once we get everything signed, the funds will be handed over to you."

I nod but remain silent. My head is pounding at this point. I never expected it would come to this.

"Do you plan on keeping the dairy farm going?" asks Jimmy. "You have more than enough land to continue producing milk while growing marijuana."

"No," I whisper. "Dairy farming has been my life, but it's on longer profitable for small operators like me."

"Then you might as well start arrangements for selling off your herd."

"It's the end of the line for McPherson's Dairy Farm," I say, slumping back onto the chair. "I hope I don't regret this."

The following week, the necessary documents are signed, and funds are provided to pay back our loans to Dominion Bank. We still have money left over for living expenses until we start selling cannabis.

***

Meryl, Sara, and I stand on the porch in silence as ten cattle transports slowly rumble across our property to the barns. Tears streak down Sara's cheek.

I step off the porch and mount the tractor parked next to the house. "Make sure Bess stays at the house. I don't want her to end up on one of the trucks. I'm going to help Jake supervise the loading." Meryl nods.

The livestock must be segregated. Some cows have been sold to a neighboring farm, but a number will be heading to a processing plant.

When I arrive at the barns, Jake is leading a group of cows into the first truck. "Jake, you take care of the mature ones. I'm going to supervise the loading of the pregnant cows and heifers."

"Are you McPherson?" asks one of the truck drivers.

"Yup. You can call me Mac."

"Do you want to show me where the heifers are?" asks the driver. "We got a couple of smaller trucks for them."

"I'll take you there now," I say, leading him to the proper barn. "We also want the pregnant cows loaded in separate trucks, so they don't get stressed."

"Gotcha," he says as he opens the gate to the pen and directs the cows to the outside of the barn. The heifers slowly climb the ramp to the front of the trailer.

It takes over two hours to load up all the animals. As each trailer is filled, the driver locks the gate and pulls out of the farm. When the last of the trucks heads off, I put a hand on one of Jake's shoulders. "There's no turning back now."

"Mr. McPherson, it feels strange seeing them leave this place."

"Yup. Things are only going to feel stranger from here on in."

"What do you mean?"

"I ain't naive. Growing marijuana was against the law a couple of years ago. People involved in this business were criminals. Now they're looked on as smart businesspeople. Scrape the surface and you might find some rot still. That's who we'll be dealing with."

"My mama won't want me working with no criminals."

I smile. "Neither does my mama."

CHAPTER 10

While Meryl readies herself for church, I had picked up the mail that had accumulated in the mailbox at our front entrance. Sitting at my desk, I grab the envelope with the logo from my friendly neighborhood bank, tearing it open and pulling out a letter.

"Meryl, listen to this," I say, poking my head into the bedroom.

"Dear, Mr. McPherson,

On behalf of the Dominion Bank of Canada, I wish to acknowledge and thank you for your prompt repayment of your commercial line of credit. We value the relationships we have with our customers and look forward to continuing to serve you and the community. Should you have future banking needs, please do not hesitate to contact me directly.

Sincerely,

Desmond Lamont, Delhi Branch Manager"

Meryl puts down her mascara brush and turns from the mirror. "That's outrageous," she says. "What a smug asshole."

"We should close all our accounts at Dominion and move them to one of the other banks in the county," I say as I ball up the letter and toss it in a wastebasket.

"Not that anyone at Dominion would actually care," she says, returning to her makeup.

"Church service starts soon," I say, looking at my watch for the twentieth time in the last fifteen minutes. "Not that I want to go. I've got a bad feeling about going."

"I'm just finishing," she replies, blotting her lipstick with a tissue. "We are going to church, end of story. We are still part of the community." It's been a couple of weeks since we were last in church, and I was not looking forward to returning today.

We arrive at the church minutes before the service begins. Delhi Baptist Church is a conservative congregation, and I don't doubt most members disapprove of the changes at our farm. I can sense it in the hushed voices around us. I lean over to whisper into Meryl's ear as the Pastor walks toward the pulpit. "If he makes any reference to marijuana, I'm out of here."

She shakes her head. "Shh."

Pastor Gabriel White gazes out at the congregation with barely a discernible smile. "I would like you to join our choir and pianist, Cindy Price, in the singing of *I Have Decided to Follow Jesus*. The hymn is in your prayer books on page thirty-eight."

The choir, dressed in black and white, reminds me of a piano keyboard. They rise from their seats as the pastor nods to Cindy to begin playing. The pastor closes his eyes and sways to the collective voices that echo through the church. When the choir is done, the members take their seats again. "That was lovely," he says, nodding in the direction of the choir.

He pulls out notes from his pocket, unfolding and spreading them out on the lectern. "In my eighteen years at Delhi Baptist Church, I've not been known as a fire and brimstone type of pastor," he says with a stone-faced expression. "But there are exceptions, and today is one of them."

I glance around the church. Children's drawings depicting scenes from Easter still decorate the yellow walls even though it's summer and the holiday is long over. It's a large crowd for this time of the year, and the hall is warm and stuffy. Large ceiling fans slowly rotate above us. Congregants fan themselves with the photocopied announcement sheets left on the seats.

"I want to talk about a pernicious substance that is creeping into our community," says Pastor White, his voice reverberating through the hall. "It goes by many names including pot, weed, reefer, herb, ganja, doobie, roach, joint, locoweed, dope, blow, and Mary Jane."

Meryl looks over at me. Her face is flushed, and she bites her lip. I look straight ahead.

"The government refers to it as cannabis," he says with a grin, dripping with sarcasm. "Almost makes it sound respectable."

"Don't be fooled by the pack of radical, godless socialists who run this country," continues the pastor, his right index finger pointing upwards. "They'll tell you it's stimulating, mind-expanding and safer to use than alcohol. Let me tell you, it's not the same as when we smoked corn silks behind the back fence."

The only other sounds in the hall are Dora Stevens' irritating nervous cough and pews creaking as congregants shift around in their seats. The usual muffled conversations and whispers during the Pastor's sermons are absent.

"Marijuana is a dangerous, intoxicating, mind-muddling drug."

"Amen!" shouts someone from the back of the hall.

"Marijuana will rot your brain. That's a fact," he says, banging his fist on the lectern. "It leads to abnormal behavior, psychological dependence, and abuse of other drugs. Our schools will be filled with stoned zombies. Grades will fall. Productivity will plummet. Remember this: the human brain is for thinking, not fumigating."

I am stunned. This is a sermon straight out of central casting. "Let's get out of here," I whisper into Meryl's ear. "This is nothing more than public shaming."

She shakes her head. "I'm not walking out and have everyone stare at us."

"The scriptures tell us, '...or do you not know that your body is a temple of the Holy Spirit within you, whom you have from God? You are not your own, for you were bought with a price. So, glorify God in your body.' Those are some pretty powerful words."

Several more amens are called out.

"Crime will fester in what was once a safe community. The local council wisely decided to ban retail marijuana stores in our community. Thank you, Mayor," says the pastor, nodding to Desmond in the first row of pews, "for doing your part to keep marijuana from becoming more accessible and out of the hands of our youth. Unfortunately, anyone with a computer can order it online like you would order a pair of work boots."

Pastor White's gaze moves away from Desmond and stops at us. "We have recently learned that a local farmer plans to grow marijuana. Right here in Norfolk County. Where our innocent kids play. Will it be safe to even drive by? Will the fumes from these farms intoxicate passersby? Is this the type of community you want? Because it's not what I have in mind for our town."

I'm pissed off. I was never a marijuana supporter, but times have changed, and I need to make a living. I expected some community resistance, but this is way over the top. My teeth are clenched, and the pounding in my ears drowns out the rest of the sermon.

"...please join the choir in singing *When We All Get to Heaven* with Cindy Price at the piano."

***

"What a pile of horseshit," I growl at Meryl as we wait in the aisle to leave the church.

Up ahead at the door is a reception line made up of the pastor along with Lucille Lamont, chair of the Women's Bible Study Group. Lucille's group doesn't limit themselves to studying the Bible. They've taken upon themselves to set and enforce an informal moral code on the community. Their past targets have included an independent bookstore, a tattoo shop, and a video game store.

I look around to determine if there's any way we can inconspicuously sneak past them. As Pastor White engages in a conversation with another congregant, I grab Meryl's arm and make my move. Keeping my head down, I slip behind another family that is waiting to shake hands with the reception line.

"Preston and Meryl, so good to see you at services," calls out Lucille.

Shit. We've been nabbed.

"Thank you," says Meryl as she turns to acknowledge Lucille. "Good to see you as well."

"Speaking of which," says Lucille, placing both her hands over Meryl's. "I haven't seen either of you at Bible study recently."

"Yes, we need to make it out again," says Meryl. I catch a glimpse of my wife out of a corner of my eye and can tell she's trying hard not to blush.

Pastor White finishes his conversation with a congregant and turns his attention to us. "Thank you for coming out to services on this fine Sunday," he says.

"How did you enjoy the pastor's sermon this morning?" asks Lucille, her gaze fixed on me.

"I didn't," I say. "Just a lot of scaremongering."

"Preston, the scriptures are God's words," says the pastor.

"While we're talking the scriptures," I say, my chest puffed out. "We don't appreciate the gossip going around town. I'm no expert on the scriptures, but I don't think they approve of gossiping behind folks' backs. Besides, what we are doing with our farm is totally legal."

"Indeed. But these are laws written by heathens," says the pastor.

"Fortunately, we live in a country where church and state are separate," I say.

I glance around and realize a growing group of congregants has formed around us, some straining to hear the conversation. Meryl senses it's time to go and grabs my hand. "You all have a wonderful Sunday," she says, pulling me out the door and down the steps of the church.

"I hope we've heard the last of this type of sermon," says Meryl, biting her lip.

"Get used to this nonsense," I say, pulling my key fob out of my pocket. "I have a sick feeling that Lucille Lamont might unleash her Bible study group on us."

CHAPTER 11

It's been three months since the herd was sold off, and we finished cannabis school. Preparations for our new enterprise are in full swing. The McPherson family is not used to sitting around idle. We're all antsy. Waiting for the construction of the new facilities to be done. Waiting for licensing. But there's still lots to do. Meryl and I have been busy interviewing people interested in working in our greenhouses and setting up the books. Sara has been helping by ordering supplies, things like plant pots and nutrients. I work with the contractor to make sure the construction is proceeding as planned. Mum has been harassing the workers. The shotguns have been locked up and out of her reach.

Staring out the living room window, I can see the nearly completed greenhouses where the barns used to sit. The glass and metal structures shimmer in the summer sun. I step outside onto the porch. It's only mid morning, but the heat and humidity are quickly climbing. There's no breeze, and the air feels exceptionally heavy. But it's also noticeably different. The heavy odor of manure is no longer around. I'd never thought it possible. The smell used to be everywhere. I swore it came out of my pores.

My phone chirps, and I pull it out of my back pocket.

"Hey, Jimmy. How's it goin', eh?"

"Hello, Preston. I've got some great news."

"I can always use some of that."

"The feds have approved your cultivating license application. You're now officially in the cannabis growing business."

"So, I guess we're making some progress. All we need is someplace to grow the stuff," I say as I look over at the partially completed greenhouses.

"That will happen soon. Didn't the construction foreman say he expects everything to be done over the next two to three weeks? You'll be ready to start up the week after Labor Day."

"Yeah, that would be good. I feel out of sorts to be honest. I'm no longer in the only business I've known but have yet to move on to something new."

"Don't you worry; you're going to be great at this. You've gone through our training program, and you have a good understanding of the business. I'll be coming around for the first month or so to answer questions and help where I can."

"I hope this works out. I still got my concerns."

"You have nothing to be concerned about. I've got to take off, Preston. Again, congratulations. Talk to you later."

"Sure thing." I hit the end button and slip the phone back into my pocket. I bound up the steps, into the house, and dash into the kitchen. Meryl is at the sink washing baking pans.

"Guess what?" I ask.

"You're applying for the Mars mission?" she answers, spinning around with a big grin.

"I'm serious," I say. "I've got big news."

"Bigger than the Mars mission?"

"Yup. We are now owners of a Health Canada cannabis producer's license."

"Mac, that's hardly big news," she says, wrapping her arms around me. "It was a given that Green Fields would be able to get us licensed, but it's good to have reached this milestone." Her wet rubber gloves drip soapy water down my back.

"Hey! You're getting me wet! You are the sloppiest hugger."

The doorbell chimes. "Are we expecting someone?" I ask, furrowing my brow.

"Nope."

"I wonder who that can be?"

Meryl pulls off her gloves and we walk over to the front door. I pull the door open to find two familiar faces.

"Mayor Lamont. Pastor White. What are you two doing here?" I ask as I feel my chest tighten and my mouth curl up into a sneer. "As if I can't guess."

"Good morning, Preston. And you, Meryl," replies the pastor. "May we come in?"

"Of course," says Meryl, stepping in front of me to let in the guests. "Excuse my appearance. I was scrubbing some pans."

Meryl leads them into the living room. I shove the door closed; maybe too hard. Desmond looks startled.

"We apologize for coming over unannounced," says Pastor White, finding a spot to sit down on one of the couches. "The subject is a tad awkward."

"Is that so?" I ask, sitting on the arm of a vacant couch, my arms crossing my chest. "Gabriel, it seems ol' Des does just fine with awkward conversations. I didn't think he would need your assistance."

"Preston, there's no need to be hostile," says Desmond, frowning. "We are here as concerned and supportive neighbors."

Meryl sits down in an armchair opposite our guests. From my perch on the arm of the couch, I look down at them. "So, why don't you tell us what's on your mind," I say, breaking the awkward silence.

"Preston and Meryl, as you know this is a traditional community," begins Desmond, his hands folded in his lap. "Your proposed cannabis farm has people upset. Maybe that's not the right word. Perhaps *concerned*."

"What would they be concerned about? No one was concerned with the tobacco farms that used to be in this county, and tobacco kills people. Besides, it's too late to turn back now. The green houses are almost finished and growing starts early September."

"As I said, we're a traditional community, and cannabis use, although now legal, is not well accepted here," says Desmond.

"I consider myself to be conservative," I spit out. "But I'm not narrow-minded or mean-spirited."

"Preston, let's try to be civil," says Gabriel.

"You know I'd still be milking cows if the community bank hadn't pulled my line of credit," I say, shooting dagger looks to Desmond.

"You know that wasn't my decision," responds Desmond. "Why are you taking it so personally?"

"Because it *is* personal, damn it!"

"If people are concerned that we are going to be selling to kids in the community, that's not going to happen," adds Meryl. "We have a growing license, not a retail license. We will be selling our crop exclusively to a company who we have a contractual agreement with. There isn't even a cannabis retailer around here, so it's not like any of our product will ever be sold in town."

"We understand all that," says Desmond, now rubbing his hands together. "It's more about the stigma. What if other farmers follow your lead? We don't want to be known as the cannabis capital of southwest Ontario. There must be something other than cannabis that you can grow on your farm."

I get up, glaring at them. "I don't give a hoot what people think. This is my farm and I'll grow what I want."

"Please, Preston, don't shoot the messenger," says Gabriel. "There's a petition going around town. Some of the ladies in the church are talking about picketing your farm and –"

The doorbell chimes again. "Excuse me," says Meryl, as she gets up and walks to the front door.

When the door opens, a familiar voice reverberates through the house. "Holy moly, I see there's some delegation here."

Meryl returns with Ferg close behind. When he catches sight of Desmond and Gabriel, he comes to a sudden halt. "Well look who's here," he says, his hands on his hips.

"I think these gentlemen are done," I say.

They both get to their feet. "You need to consider what we've talked about," says Desmond. "We're hoping to keep some harmony in the community."

My face turns bright red. "We obviously have different views on how to achieve harmony. Mine is to accept my right to grow what I want on my farm. If it was up to you, I would go broke and sell the farm!"

"Thank you for dropping by," says Meryl as she leads them to the door. "Say hi to Lucille for me."

Ferg plops down on the vacated couch. "What a pair of buggers they are."

"They say some ladies at the church are looking to set up some protests in front of the property," I say. "No doubt Lucille and her band of Bible thumpers are behind this. The Lamonts really have it out for us."

"I heard that too. What are you fixing to do?"

"Nothing. I don't like the idea of some tight-ass town folks telling me what I can grow on my property. Fuck 'em."

"You should be thinking about hiring some security for this place," says Ferg. "I know some guys who -"

"Hell, you always know some guy," I say, shaking my head. "We'll be fine. I'm not too worried about some Bible thumpers."

"I'm just sayin' you need to protect your investment in case some kook tries to start some trouble."

CHAPTER 12

I stand at the entrance of the greenhouse we call the mother room, admiring the marijuana plants gently swaying to the breeze created by the overhead fans. New marijuana plants are cloned from plants in the mother room, which are never allowed to flower. The sun streaming through the glass ceiling and walls illuminate the blackish green plant leaves. I pick one of the thin jagged leaves and hold it to my nose. There's almost no scent.

Despite it being a cool fall day, its feels like early summer inside. The climate control system, along with the fans, simulates ideal outdoor growing conditions all year long, without having to deal with pests and bad weather.

"Morning, Dad." I turn around and see Sara, letting out a muffled yawn.

"Mornin'," I say. "Where's Jake?"

"He was right behind me."

I look down the roadway and see our farmhand shuffling toward the greenhouse. "C'mon, Jake," I call out. "Let's get a move on."

As he approaches, he sheepishly replies, "Sorry, Mr. McPherson."

"You people are getting soft now that you no longer have to get up early to milk cows," I say. I push a supply cart to the start of a row of plants. "You should know by now how the cloning works."

The other two nod their heads.

"Good," I say, grabbing a stack of pots and nutrient pucks and placing them on a small, wheeled cart. "Sarah, you and I will take a couple cuttings from each plant. Make sure to use the fastest growing points."

"I got this, Dad," says Sara. "Just like in cannabis school."

"If you notice a mother plant not doing well, pull it aside," I say. "Jimmy is coming by and he'll take a look at them."

"What about me?" asks Jake.

I wheel a cart with trays in his direction. "Your job is to make sure the clones are properly planted in the pots," I say. "Then put the covers over the trays and take them into the cloning room."

"You got it, Mr. McPherson."

"Make sure that the covers are on tight," I say. "Otherwise, the humidity level in the trays will be too low for the roots to grow."

Jake grabs the cart from me then stops and looks back at me. "I still don't understand how come there ain't no daddy plants."

"The daddies don't produce flowers, so they're of no use to us," I say, shaking my head.

"It's all so confusing to me still. I used to think people smoked the leaves."

"Think of it like a corn plant. We don't eat the leaves, only the seeds."

Starting at one end of a row, I examine the first plant. Looking over the plant, I spot a perfect branch and grab my shears off my cart to snip it off at a forty-five-degree angle. I nestle the cutting into a nutrient puck at the bottom of a pot. I work my way down the row of plants, repeating the process.

"Hey, Mac. This looks like a busy squad," says a familiar voice, bouncing off the greenhouse walls.

I look back at the entrance where Jimmy is leaning against the door with his hands in his pockets.

"Jake, you're on your own for a while," I say, marching toward the entrance.

"What a great setup. I see you have your indica plants on this side and sativa growing on the other side," says Jimmy, stooping down to examine the leaves on a few plants. He burrows his finger into some of the pots to check the moisture of the soil.

"You know your stuff."

"I don't think I ever mentioned how I got started in the business. When I was a teen, I was growing some plants for my dad. He had a prescription for medical marijuana, and to save him money, I grew four plants which was the legal limit. Then some of his buddies with prescriptions asked me to grow for them too. The next thing I know I've got this productive weed farm."

"So, your experience was always on the legit side?" I ask.

"Not quite," responds Jimmy. "I learned a lot and was developing some fantastic strains. Then I was approached by a grow-op in British Columbia and was asked to work on their cultivation program. I was twenty-four years old, and interested in the cannabis culture, so I said sure. Worked there for a couple of years until legalization. Got hired by Green Fields last year."

Jimmy watches Jake and Sara slowly work their way down the greenhouse. "Are these the only people you have working?"

"I have a couple of other people that I recently hired. Once we have more plants, and all the vegetation and flowering rooms going, we'll add a few more."

"Let me check the enviros," he says, looking over the climate control display panel set up on a wall close to the entrance. Jimmy punches a few buttons and looks at the numbers displayed.

"How is it looking?" I ask.

"Pretty good. The temp is bang on. I think the humidity is too high, though. I don't want to see mold forming on your herbs."

"What do you suggest I do?"

"Just turn down the flow in the drip lines going to the pots. When the plants get more water than they can absorb, the excess evaporates, increasing the humidity in the room."

"Sounds easy enough."

"Like they said during training, growing weed is easy," says Jimmy. "Keep up the pruning. You want your plants to have a lollipop shape. I'll come by every two weeks for a few months to check and see if everything is growing as they should."

"We're setting up the nursery and plan on cloning every week," I say. "Do you want to see the room?"

"Not today," he responds. "What I would like to see are your records. Both the federal and provincial governments will be poking their noses in here, and I want to make sure you're ready for them."

***

Jimmy stares intently at the computer monitor while Meryl and I look on. He grips the computer mouse with his right hand, while the other hand is finger tapping on my desktop. "Everything seems to be set up properly," he says.

"I used the templates you provided us," says Meryl.

Footsteps pound up the porch steps, and the front door bangs open. We turn toward the door of my office when Jake flies into the room breathing heavily.

"Mr. McPherson...we got us a problem," says Jake between gasps for air.

"What's going on?" I ask, frowning.

"It's Bess...she got into the mother room...and been eating plants."

"Oh crap!" I holler. "I told you to keep the doors to the greenhouses shut."

"I swear it was an accident."

"Is Bess okay?" asks Meryl.

"She's acting kinda peculiar," says Jake, his face still flushed. "She might be stoned or something."

"I doubt she could be high," says Jimmy, getting up from his seat. "There's only negligible amounts of THC in the leaves, and none of the mother plants have buds."

"I'm heading over to the greenhouse to see how much damage she did," I say.

I shut down the laptop and we follow Jake back to the greenhouse. About two-thirds of the way there, we pass Bess, who pretends not to see us. I walk in front of her and look her straight in the eyes. "You stay out of the greenhouses," I say firmly. "Do you hear me?"

"Mooooo."

Bess plods her way back to the house while we continue toward the greenhouses. As we approach, I can see the door to the mother room is wide open.

"Goddamn it, Jake," I say, shaking my fist. "The door is *still* not closed. There are days when I wonder whether you could pour water out of a boot with instructions on the heel."

"Sorry, Mr. McPherson," says Jake as he scrambles ahead to shut it.

"Mac, don't be rude," says Meryl.

The mother room is in worse shape than I had expected. Several pots have been knocked over, damaging the plants and spilling soil onto the floor. Other plants have been chewed on. The last thing I need is a weed-loving cow on the property.

"Whoa! The only pests I've ever come across were mites and gnats," says Jimmy. "Cows are a first for me."

"Let's start cleaning this mess up," I say, picking up a couple of pots off the floor.

"I'll get a broom to sweep up the dirt," says Jake.

"And shut the door behind you," I remind him.

"You need to do a count of damaged plants," says Jimmy. He walks over and stoops to pick up a pot that is on its side. "Make sure to incinerate the plants that can't be salvaged and update the database."

"For sure," says Meryl.

"I know I'm repeating myself, but the government inspectors will expect that you can account for every single plant."

"Seriously, every plant?" I ask, grimacing. "Are they really such tight-asses?"

"They are," responds Jimmy. "The government is being heavy-handed because they need to reassure the public that they're in control. Make sure your inventory is as tight as can be."

Jesus Murphy, I can hardly wait to have one of the inspectors show up at the farm. I'm guessing they won't find a weed-eating cow that funny.

CHAPTER 13

The meeting room in the church basement has about fifteen women milling about. It's a drab room with beige-painted walls made of cinderblocks and a yellowed tile ceiling. Two dozen plastic stacking chairs are arranged theater-style facing the front the room. Several women are lined up at a folding table against one of the side walls, waiting their turn to grab a cup of coffee and a couple of cookies.

Lucille Lamont is chatting with two women when, out of the corner of her eye, she catches Pastor White entering the room. She excuses herself and rushes over. "Good evening, Pastor. So good of you to join us."

"My pleasure," he says, nodding his head to a few of the women close by. "Thank you so much for organizing this. It's quite a large undertaking."

"This is a serious matter and, as you know, Desmond and I care deeply about the community," she says, her head raised and chin jutting out. "It's a little past eight o'clock. Are you ready to begin?"

The pastor nods. Lucille moves to the front of the room and clears her throat loud enough to be heard above the collective chatter. "Could everyone please take your seats?" Her request triggers the gathering to move toward vacant chairs. When everyone is seated, she continues. "I would like to thank everyone for coming out tonight. As you can see, Pastor White has kindly taken time from his busy schedule to join us. He has a few words he would like to say."

The pastor stands up to address the group. "I want to thank our dedicated chair, Lucille Lamont, and all of you in our Bible study group. I know you share my concern over cannabis legalization and the associated moral decline of our society. Your efforts will send a message that we are more than ready to defend our community. The scriptures tell us to be alert and of sober mind. Your enemy, the devil, prowls around like a roaring lion, looking for some to devour." He sits back down as the women break out into applause, and he acknowledges them with a wave of a hand.

All eyes return to Lucille. "We all know why we are here tonight," she says. "The cannabis farm run by the McPhersons is a blight on our community." She pauses and watches heads nodding in the audience.

"Is there anything we can do about it?" someone shouts.

"Indeed. I have a plan," says Lucille, puffing out her chest. "We are going to picket the farm." A murmur spreads through the room.

"What's the point of that?" asks a woman in the front row.

"I'm glad you asked, Anne Marie," responds Lucille, as a smile spreads across her face. "My plan is to have the picket line stop cars from entering the farm. Over time, we will drive them right out of business."

Everyone in the room is talking at once. A woman near the back has her hand up. "Do you have a question, Edna?"

The woman sheepishly rises. "For the picket to be effective, won't we need to be picketing every day? We don't have enough people here, and I can't be marching in front of the farm seven days a week." The noise in the room picks up as discussions break out.

Lucille raises her hands in front of her and the chatter settles down. "I've taken that into consideration in my planning. We will start with pickets one or two days a week. Meanwhile, I will be reaching out to neighbouring communities, other churches, and anti-drug groups for volunteers to join us. We are going to set up a website where people can sign up for shifts. In a few months, I hope to have pickets operating all day long, seven days a week."

A woman in the second row shoots up onto her feet. "I can get my son, Sean, to help with the website. He's good at those things."

"Splendid!" responds Lucille. "Now, who is ready to sign up for picket duty?"

Every hand in the room goes up.

CHAPTER 14

"Hey, Mac, how's it goin', eh?"

I look up from the plant I'm trimming. "Ferg, you ain't been around here in ages," I say, smirking. "Afraid you might find something illegal going on?"

"Come on, Mac. You know we've been short-staffed. I've been doing extra shifts."

"Damn, that must mean coffee and donut sales are up at Tim Hortons."

"Stop busting my chops," he says, looking down at my bag of plant trimmings. "Why the heck are you cutting off all these branches? Ain't you gonna have fewer buds to pick?"

I drag my bag to the next plant. "You don't know the first thing about growing weed. It's like pruning any plant. This is how you produce the healthiest plants and the biggest buds."

"None of these plants have any buds."

"Yup, these plants are kept from flowering because they're the mothers," I say. "We've been growing for over two months, and we finally have some plants with flowers. I plan to give everyone a tour of the operations before the family meeting tonight, but you can get an advance preview."

"Sure, if you got the time."

"First we need to get you into some protective gear."

"Protective gear? Are you worried I'm going to get stoned walking around here?"

I lead him back to the entrance. "It's to protect my crop," I say, pulling out a pair of booties from a box on the shelf next to the door. "Your boots could be carrying all kinds of nasty bugs. I'm not supposed to be using any pesticides, so I need to protect my investment."

After he slips on the booties, I hand him a white lab coat. "Jesus Murphy," says Ferg, gawking at the coat. "Next you'll be handing me a hazmat suit."

"We run an organic operation, but some farms do have them. We also use gloves when handling the plants," I say, holding out my gloved hands.

"This coat is too small," Ferg complains, struggling to do up all the buttons.

"I think the problem is that your gut is too big," I joke, poking my finger into his belly. I grab another coat and toss it to him. "Try this one on. We have it here for Bess when she wanders into the greenhouses."

"Okay, I could afford to lose a couple of pounds but I'm not that big."

We wander down the aisle between two rows of potted plants. "We call this the mother room. We don't grow new plants from seeds; takes too long. Instead, we keep a greenhouse full of plants that are only used for cloning."

"Where are the fathers?"

I let out a sigh. "Why does everyone ask the same dumb question?"

"Why is it a dumb question?"

"Ferg, I ran a dairy farm. Did you ever see any bulls running around here?"

"Bulls don't produce milk."

"Exactly. And male plants don't produce buds."

"Oh."

"After about six months, each mother plant is replaced with one of its clones and destroyed."

"Why do they have to be replaced?" asks Ferg as he bends down to examine a plant up close.

"After a while, the mothers begin to degrade," I say. "Then the clones won't be as strong. I'm going to use the dairy farm analogy. You know, like when we would sell off a cow after about six years when her milk production drops. Older plants aren't going to produce strong baby plants after a while."

"Gotcha."

"We pick the fastest growing branches for clones," I say, reaching down to grab a branch of the closest plant. "Something like this one."

"How do you keep the moms from flowering?"

"By controlling the amount of light in here. I'll show you how that's done shortly."

We head back to the door. "Drop your booties in the garbage pail."

Ferg bends over to slip a bootie off and almost topples over.

We step outside into light snow flurries. The snow crunches beneath our boots as we walk to the next greenhouse. "We're not going to go inside the cloning room," I say as we stop in front of the door. "It's pretty humid inside, and I don't want your uniform to get all sweaty."

"Very funny," says Ferg, peering through the glass walls.

"Not only are the cuttings grown in high humidity, but the lighting is jacked up to twenty-two hours each day."

"It's like an incubator."

"Pretty much," I agree. "After about a month, the clones are big enough to be transplanted and moved into a vegetation room."

"So, does each greenhouse have a different purpose?"

"Some are the same," I say as we walk to another structure. I pull the door open for my brother-in-law. The sun streams through the glass roof, illuminating the dense green canopy produced by the tightly packed rows of plants. "And this is one of our vegetation rooms."

"Looks the same as the mother room to me."

I grab new booties and give one set to Ferg. "There's not much difference," I say, pulling on a pair of booties over my shoes. "These plants aren't cloned. We trim off lower and side growth, so that most growth is concentrated upward. Plants grow to about four feet."

"They're not even close to that height."

"How it works is that when the plants hit about two-and-a-half feet, that will be the end of the vegetation stage and we allow them to flower. That takes about six to eight weeks."

"You sound like a florist," says Ferg, snickering. "Does that mean you have to move all these plants again?"

"Nope. Flowering is triggered by a drop in the amount of light the plants receive. We will cut back on the lighting from eighteen hours a day to about twelve, and this greenhouse will become a flowering room."

"That's pretty cool," says Ferg, strolling through the greenhouse. "That's all there is to it?"

"It is simple," I say, "but since it's all about the yields, you want to create ideal growing conditions. Like we used to monitor the cows, we have to monitor the plants and the greenhouse. To prevent pests, it's important to control the temperature and humidity and provide proper ventilation."

"You know this is going to impress the hell out of Graham," says Ferg.

As I lock the greenhouse door and activate the alarm, we hear what sounds like a moo coming from one of the other greenhouses. We scoot over to the nursery and find the door wide open. Inside, Bess is casually chewing on a plant. "Damn it, Bess! Stay out of the greenhouses!"

***

Family meetings have been less than cordial this past year. Lower profits and cash flow problems have created tension. I procrastinate at starting the meeting, sitting silently as I scan the room. Sara is zoned into her phone and oblivious to what is going on around the table. Meryl and Graham are discussing politics. "If the government doesn't take control of our debt," remarks Graham, jabbing a finger in Meryl's direction, "this country will soon be a basket case."

Meryl shakes her head, her voice rising in volume. "The country can't be run based on what would be good for corporations and investors. We need to preserve our social programs and take care of people." Their 'discussions' always evolve into arguments.

Ferg is describing a recent police incident to Uncle Liam and Mum, complete with his usual embellishment. "We got a call a few weeks ago from Gibby's Hardware that someone had held them up at gunpoint. We got a description of the perp from the staff and a couple of customers, and a bad video from a security camera. There weren't any other leads. No one even saw the car he was driving."

"You know he was probably not local," Liam suggests.

"Yeah, we kind of figured out pretty quickly. A week goes by, and someone calls the office. They had seen a Facebook post with a photo of a guy holding a gun and a wad of cash. The caption said 'Bad hombre. Gibby's. Done.' I mean, could he have made it easier?" Ferg breaks into a loud cackle that fills the room. "You should have seen his face when we made a visit to his place the next day." I've already heard this story twice. Changes each time.

The room is decorated for the holiday with tinsel, red and green candles, and Christmas figurines. An oversized Christmas tree in the adjoining living room twinkles in the corner. Despite the season, dread always permeates the room at the start of every family meeting. When I'm looking for support, I inevitably get criticism. When I need advice, I'm more likely to get blank stares. The group was relatively subdued during the walk through the facility. I'm not sure what that means.

I clear my throat. "We should get started. Some of you have a long drive home." The room goes quiet, apart from Ferg who is still laughing at his story.

"Before we start," says Liam, stirring sugar into his cup of tea, "I have to admit you got an impressive operation here, Mac."

"Thanks," I say, letting a small smile spread across my face. "I wanted the family to see how much we've progressed. It was a smoother transition from dairy than expected. But this wouldn't have been possible without the help from the people at Green Fields."

"Enough with the speeches," says Mum. Crumbs of partially chewed coffee cake fly out of her mouth. "When do we get to the main course?"

"Mum, you've already had dinner," I say. "We're discussing the family farm."

"Oh, really?" she asks while pouring tea into her cup, spilling some on the tablecloth. "What happened to all the cows? Did someone forget to close the barn doors?"

"I told you, we sold the cows," I say with a sigh.

"And what's with all this talk about weeds? Fortunately, your father isn't around to see how neglected the farm has become. No cows, no crops, just weeds sprouting everywhere. It's a disgrace!"

Graham coughs up his tea.

I reach over to pat her hand. "Mum, we aren't growing those kinds of weeds. The farm isn't being neglected."

"I think this all worked out great, just like I said it would," says Ferg. He reaches across the table for another slice of cake.

"I need to discuss the state of our bottom line," I say as my smile fades away. "The cannabis industry is still young and evolving. There are lots of small growers like us. The market has quickly gone from undersupply to oversupply."

Meryl distributes copies of the financial report around the table.

"Does that mean you're having problems selling your product?" asks Graham as he flips through the report.

"No. Green Fields is providing us with access to markets," I reply. "But prices are falling, and some product has been returned unsold."

"So, what you're telling us is that you've gone from losing money producing milk to losing money growing weed?" asks Graham.

"No, we aren't losing money. But we're not making as much as we had hoped to."

Sara jumps in. "But we aren't yet at full production. There are opportunities to improve profitability, right Dad?"

"There are. Electricity costs are high. In the next quarter, the days get longer, which means we will be using more natural sunlight and less artificial lighting. I've been looking into alternatives to the high-pressure sodium lights used in our greenhouses. We may convert to LED lighting eventually. Installing solar panels would help a lot, but the technology is pricy, and the payback period is long."

"Also, our yields have been lower than expected," says Meryl. "Our initial crop produced smaller flowers and too much moisture, which also impacted on price. As we become more experienced, we will be able to generate more product per square-foot of greenhouse space."

"I thought the stuff was supposed to be so easy to grow," says Graham. The smirk and his tone are condescending.

"It is easy enough to grow," I say, "but there's a learning curve if you want to become a high-volume producer."

"Which gets me back to my case for selling off some of the excess land," says Graham.

"Graham, that's all you ever want to do," complains Sara. "Sell off the family legacy."

"Because it's the most prudent thing to do."

"Mac," says Liam. "You know he's right."

I get off my seat, leaning forward with my hands on the table for support. "Must I remind you that agriculture is the backbone of this country? Farmers put up with random weather, lurking pestilence, and pollution to protect our land and ensure that Canadians have fresh, safe, and healthy produce to eat. We have been -"

Graham has a pinched expression as he rolls his eyes. "You can drop your farm speech. You aren't feeding Canadians anymore."

Meryl jumps to her feet. "Bitch, bitch, bitch. That's all some of you do. Meanwhile, we are working our butts off. We were forced by external circumstances to make a seismic change in our business. You haven't even given us a chance to succeed. How about acting like a family and showing some support?"

"She's right," I say. "It's way too early to be throwing in the towel. We just started. We can make this thing work." I gaze around the table, and the body language says it all. This is going to be a fight every step of the way.

Graham shakes his head. "Look, there's too much competition. There's a lot of big players that have jumped into the market with huge growing capacity. All you've done is gone from being a small dairy operator to a small cannabis operator. But I'm sure someone would be happy to buy this place."

"Graham, if I've said it once, I've said it a thousand times," I say, gripping the pen in my hand so tightly it snaps in two. "I'm not selling this farm!"

Graham dismissively waves his hand in the air. "Alright, let's see how this plays out. All this money has already been sunk into this place. Mac, you're going to have to improve your profit margins."

CHAPTER 15

I roll out of bed as the sun begins to peek through the edges of the window blind in our bedroom. One huge advantage that the weed farm has over the dairy farm is that we get to wake up at a decent hour. It took me a long time to stop waking up at 4:00 a.m. for that first milking of the day.

After a quick breakfast, I throw on a winter coat and a pair of boots and step outside. The wind is whipping around the fallen snow, creating white powdery clouds drifting across the property. Despite the frigid weather, I decide to walk to the greenhouses, pulling the hood to my coat tight to keep my head warm.

As is the pattern, I'm the first to arrive at the start of the workday. I unlock the door to greenhouse three and quickly close it to keep out the cold. I hear a splashing sound and look down at my feet. I'm standing in two inches of water. *Mother of God, what happened?!*

I scramble over to the water valve feeding the drip line and, sure enough, the connection is off. Water is pouring out of the spout onto the greenhouse floor. I quickly shut off the water and wade over to the climate control display panel. No surprise, the humidity level is alarmingly high. The flooding should have triggered an alarm on my phone. I pull out my phone and realize I have it shut off.

"What the hell happened?"

I turn to the entrance and see a stunned Sara staring at me. "A flood is what happened. Who was working in here yesterday? I bet it was Jake."

"I was here, Mr. McPherson," responds Jake who standing behind Sara. "Gosh, I got no clue how this happened, though."

"*You* happened," I say, with a flash of anger. "It's like a rainforest in here."

"I guess I might have knocked the connection loose with a cart or something," Jakes mumbles, avoiding eye contact. "We can let it dry up, right?"

"No, we can't," I answer, my face now inches away from Jake's. "Before you know it, the greenhouse is going to be wall-to-wall mold. The marijuana plants will be toast."

"What should we do?" asks Sara.

I pull out my phone. "Don't know, so I better call Jimmy."

"Hey, Preston, what's going on?"

"Sorry to call you so early in the day but we have a situation here."

"What kind of situation? Don't tell me your cow has been snacking on plants again."

"No, but we've got a flood in greenhouse three."

"How much water are we talking about?"

"Enough that we could go water skiing!"

"Calm down. Your plants are off the ground, so unless it's two feet deep, there's no immediate damage. I'll swing by later this morning with some equipment to help clean up."

"Thanks a lot, Jimmy. See ya later."

I walk toward the entrance where Jake is staring at me with his mouth wide open. "What is it?"

"I was thinking I can get a mop and bucket and start sopping up the water."

I take a deep breath. "Son, you can't mop up this much water. Why don't you go and work in greenhouse five today? And try to keep out of trouble."

***

About two hours later, Jimmy arrives in a large box van with an assistant. Instead of his usual business suit, Jimmy is wearing jeans and rubber boots.

"Hi Preston, this is Dale," he says, swinging open the rear hatch of the van. "He's got experience with cleaning up water damage."

"Nice to meet you," I say. "And much appreciate your help."

I help unload the equipment from the back of the van. "This looks like a big wet/dry vacuum," I say, pointing at a large gray machine.

"That's exactly what it is," responds Dale, pushing the machine through the greenhouse door. "It's a water extractor but works the same way. This will suck up twenty gallons per minute. Perfect for a big job like this."

Once inside, he turns the machine on and pushes the extractor down one of the aisles. Despite the chilly air, Jimmy and I step outside to get away from the loud hum from the equipment. "You've had some bad breaks already," says Jimmy, stomping his feet to keep warm. "First your weed-loving cow and now the flood."

"Yeah, let's hope this is the end of it."

A couple of minutes pass and Dale pulls the extractor out of the greenhouse. He empties the water reservoir and heads back inside. In a little over an hour, most of the water is sucked out of the greenhouse, and a patch of ice big enough to be used as a skating rink forms next to the structure. We load the extractor back into the van and carry several large fans into the wet greenhouse.

"Leave things running for couple of days and keep an eye on the humidity level," Dale instructs. "I'll be back at the end of the week to pick up the fans."

I thank them again as the pull away. I hope this is the end of our problems.

CHAPTER 16

While unloading plastic plant pails from my truck outside the greenhouses, two identical white panel vans pull up next to me. The names painted on the doors tell me that I've got inspectors from two government agencies visiting. The drivers step out of their vans and walk toward me. They're both under forty, dressed in jeans and khaki winter parkas. One is tall with red hair and a neatly trimmed beard. The shorter guy is slightly overweight with a shaved head.

A big knot forms in my gut. I knew this day was coming, but now that it's here, I need to force myself from freaking out. "Can I help you fellas?"

"We're looking for Preston McPherson," says the short guy with a piercing stern look.

"That would be me."

"I'm Glen Fleming, an inspector from the Ontario Cannabis Agency."

"And I'm Phil Garneau, an inspector from the federal Department of Health."

They both hand me business cards, and Garneau reads a prepared statement regarding government inspection policy and my legal rights and obligations. It feels more like I'm being arrested and they're reading me my rights.

"Welcome," I say, shaking their hands. I hope they don't notice my sweaty palms. "Do you always carry out inspections together?"

"We try to coordinate our visits," replies Fleming.

Unfriendly – check. Humorless – check. Robotic – check. This is going to be a fun day.

"And why is the Ontario Cannabis Agency inspecting me?" I ask, staring at their business cards. "I don't sell any product to you guys. It all goes to Green Fields."

"Because we control the distribution of cannabis in the province," says Fleming, pointing to a page of their inspection policy document. "We need to ensure that everything that is legally grown remains in the distribution network."

"Gotcha. Well, where would you like to start?"

"I need to take plant samples for testing," says Garneau. He walks back to his van and removes a black vinyl case from the trunk.

"Then follow me," I say, leading them to the first greenhouse. "This is our mother room."

"Take us to your vegetation and flowering rooms," says Garneau. His sharp tone causes the back of my neck to sweat now. I counter the reaction with a forced smile.

"Sure thing," I say as we move on to the next greenhouse. "Did you have any problems finding the farm?"

"No," says Fleming.

When we get to the first vegetation room, the inspectors pull off their parkas and grab protective gear kept by the door. Fleming flips open his case and pulls out a cutting tool and some sample bags. He walks up an aisle and stops every so often to cut off a shoot and place it in a bag, which he labels with a Sharpie. Garneau examines the climate control display panel, writing down notes in a journal.

Sara walks into the greenhouse and heads directly toward me. "Who are these guys?" she whispers.

"Government inspectors."

"Oh, shit. Is everything alright?"

"Hope so," I say, frowning.

Garneau returns with his filled sample bags and places them in his case. "We're ready to move on to the next greenhouse," he says.

"Sure thing."

They follow the same routine in each greenhouse, taking samples and notes but saying nothing. These guys are strictly business and about as friendly as a pair of tree stumps.

After exiting the last greenhouse, we walk back to our vehicles. "Thanks for coming by," I say. "If there's anything else I can do for you, just let me know."

"We're not done yet," say Fleming, abruptly.

"What else is there?"

"We need to see your business records."

"Oh yeah, sure," I say. "Follow me back to the house."

We each get into our vehicles. I grab my phone and call Meryl.

"What's up?"

"I'm on my way home with a couple of government inspectors," I say, gripping the steering wheel so tight my knuckles turn white. "They want to see our records."

"That's not a problem. Everything is in order."

"These guys make me nervous. As careful as we've been, I'm still worried they'll uncover something."

"Just relax. We'll be fine."

Snow begins to fall as we follow the road back to the house. I park my truck in front of the porch and the two vans pull up next to me. I rush to the front door to let them in. Mum is in the living room watching a soap, wearing a formal dress.

"Mum, why are you dressed up?" I ask.

"For the wedding," she says, pointing to the TV. "Alex and Cindi are tying the knot. I think she's making a big mistake. He's a scoundrel and a cheat. I predict they won't make it through the first year." She looks up and realizes there are guests. "Who are these fine-looking gentlemen?" she asks, getting up from her seat.

"They're government inspectors, Mum," I say.

"Would you boys like to sit down for some tea and watch the wedding?" she asks, batting her eyelashes.

"Just show us where you keep your records," says Fleming.

"Sure," I say. "Follow me."

As we stroll down the hall, Mum calls out, "You know that Cindi is pregnant. It's the only reason they're getting married. He doesn't love her."

I lead them into my office. Meryl is in front of the computer, pulling up reports. "This is my wife Meryl, who is also our business manager. She'll provide you with any info you need."

"For a start, we need to see your sales report, a printout of your purchases, an inventory report, nutrients and chemical reports, and all your test results," says Garneau.

Meryl continues to print reports for the inspectors while I sit in the corner of the room. I try to remain calm, but my gut is in turmoil. They fire a lot of questions at Meryl, which she responds to in a professional manner. After about forty minutes, they have everything they need and pack up.

"How did we do?" I ask, biting my lip. "Everything is in order, right?"

"Not exactly," says Garneau, as he hands me a copy of his inspection to sign.

"What do you mean by not exactly?" I ask, the pen shaking as I sign the report.

"Our records are consistent with the plant counts in the greenhouses," says Meryl.

Fleming takes back one copy of the signed inspection report. "You have suspicious inventory losses related to a cow. Highly unusual."

"But that's exactly what happened," I explain. "Our pet cow, Bess, seems to enjoy munching on the plants. She keeps getting into the greenhouses."

"We're going to be recommending your inspection cycle be accelerated," adds Garneau. "We'll leave you a copy of our on-site report. A more detailed report will follow in the mail once we get the results back from the lab."

As they drive away from the property, I'm still holding the report in my hand. I turn to Meryl. "Jesus Murphy! I can't wait to do this again."

CHAPTER 17

I'm about to settle down in front of the TV for the evening when I hear the voice activated alarm in the kitchen "ALARM ACTIVATION IN ZONE FOUR...ALARM ACTIVATION IN ZONE FOUR..."

Looking across the room at Meryl, who is reading, I mumble, "Not another damn activation." I get up and stroll to the kitchen to reset the alarm. This is the third activation this month. Hopefully, it's another false alarm. We've heard that several cannabis greenhouses in the Hamilton region have experienced break-ins recently. Every time the alarm goes off, my gut blows up on me. I search for some antacid tablets in a kitchen drawer.

"Another racoon causing mischief?" Meryl calls out, placing the book onto her lap.

"Let's hope so," I respond, grabbing a torch light, a jacket, and boots. "I always get a little paranoid when it's one of the flowering rooms."

"I'm sure it's a false alarm."

As I step onto the porch, the crisp May evening air sends a shiver through me. Pulling out the key fob in my jacket pocket, I unlock my truck and climb into the cab. In the distance, the brightly lit greenhouses illuminate the way.

I park next to the greenhouse where the alarm was activated and pull out the shotgun stowed behind my seat. Unlike the other greenhouses, this one is dark because the lights shut off early in the flowering rooms. The beam from the torch light strikes the door, or what is left of it. The ground around it is covered with shards of glass. Gripping the shotgun, maybe too tightly, I carefully pull the door open, step into the greenhouse and switch on the lights. I slowly creep up and down the aisle with the gun's stock tight against my body and my index finger touching the trigger.

When I'm satisfied there's no one in the greenhouse, I exhale and relax my grip on the gun. What a mess, though. Someone has pulled plants out of pots and carried them off. There's spilled soil everywhere. I walk over to the climate control display panel to ensure the greenhouse environment is still stable before shutting off the lights and returning to the truck. The shotgun goes back onto the rack behind the seats. Reaching into my jacket, I pull out my phone.

"Hey Ferg, I got a problem here. I need you to come over."

"What's up, Mac?"

"Someone's broken into one of the greenhouses."

"Anything stolen?"

"A whole shit-load of plants."

"I'll be right over."

I wait in the truck for Ferg to show up. The lights in the other greenhouses shut off, leaving the area in darkness. I turn on the truck lights so Ferg can find his way. Several minutes later, I see him manoeuvring his cruiser up our roadway. He's got his blue and red emergency lights flashing. Ferg always goes overboard.

He pulls up behind my truck and shuts off his vehicle. His boots crunch the gravel as he approaches my truck. I shove open the door and get out.

"What's with the flashing lights? This isn't a national emergency."

"Bite me," says Ferg, hiking up his pants. "Let's take a look and see what we got here."

We walk over to the greenhouse, and he points his flashlight at the door to examine it. "Looks like they used a crowbar to pry open the door."

"No shit, Inspector Clouseau."

He uses his boot to push aside the half-opened door and steps inside. I follow and turn the lights back on. "I don't want the lights on too long because this room houses flowering plants. At least what's left of the plants."

"Do I need to put on the booties?" he asks, grinning.

"Don't worry about it. This greenhouse is already fucked up."

"Looks like whoever pulled this off grabbed as many plants as they could before you would show up," says Ferg, trying to step around a clump of soil on the concrete floor. "They probably stuffed them into green garbage bags."

"Any chance you can catch who did this?" I ask.

"I can send one of the guys over in the morning to check for evidence," he says. "Don't clean up the mess until we've investigated. Do you have surveillance cameras set in here?"

"Yeah, I do."

Ferg has his notebook and jotting down a few details for his incident report. "That might help. We'll take a look tomorrow."

"I hope you can nab the bastards!"

I walk through the room, counting the empty pots. "I count nineteen missing plants," I say, frowning. "I guess it could have been worse."

"How much product does that come out to?"

"An awful lot. I estimate about forty pounds of weed. Oh crap; this is going to turn out to be a sixty-thousand-dollar loss. As if I can afford this right now."

"Whoa!" says Ferg, letting out a whistle. "Doesn't your insurance cover this?"

"Partly. I've got a big deductible."

"You need to upgrade your security."

"I should," I say as we head out the door. I instinctively try to lock the door before remembering it's broken. "Green Fields only recommended an alarm system and video cameras. Looks like I could use a guard or two."

"That's better than taking losses like this."

"I should do another count before I update the inventory," I say. "Inspectors were in last week and were all over our inventory. They made a big stink about Bess' snacking habit."

"That gives me a thought," says Ferg as he slides behind the wheel of his cruiser.

I yank open the passenger door of the cruiser to get away from the chilly night air. "Oh shit, not another one of your thoughts."

Ferg stuffs his notebook into a coat pocket. "Hear me out. Let's say you report that forty plants were stolen."

I place my hands in front of the heating vents to warm them. "Why would I do that?"

"You're complaining that prices have been dropping and cutting into your profits, right?"

"Yeah."

"Prices south of the border are higher than Canada. If you were to find a buyer for the extra 'missing' plants, you could replace all of that sixty-thousand-dollar loss. If that buyer is in the U.S., where prices are higher, you should be able to walk away with a nice profit plus collect whatever the insurance company pays you for the claim."

"What do you mean extra missing plants?" I ask, absent-mindedly rubbing my chin. "Are you suggesting that I exaggerate the loss?"

"Mac, people do it all the time."

"And I'm not allowed to sell to anyone else except Green Fields," I say, shaking my head. "I'd be in breach of my contract and would lose my growing license."

"Only if you get caught."

"This is crazy talk. Besides, I don't know any American buyers. And it would mean smuggling weed over the border, which we both know is risky and illegal. Do you need anymore reasons to drop the idea?"

"At least think about it. I'm sure I can come up with a plan. We can make this work."

"The answer will still be no," I say, throwing my head back against my headrest. "I'm too tired to listen to this shit. And I could use a drink."

"I don't have a bottle in the car, but I have this," say Ferg, pulling a joint out of his shirt pocket.

"What the fuck is that?"

"What does it look like?"

"A marijuana cigarette."

"Bingo!" Ferg exclaims, pulling on an imaginary cord. "What's with the weird look? You know it's legal now?"

I grab the joint out of his hand. "Yeah, I know. So, where did you get it?"

"We shut down an illegal dispensary in Simcoe last month, and not all of the inventory made it to our evidence room," he says with a wink.

"Then that stuff is illegal."

"How can you tell? It all looks the same."

"You can legally buy it, but you decide to steal some instead." What a piece of work. Next, he'll be offering me a big screen TV that happened to have fallen off some truck.

"I prefer not to have a record of my weed purchases, if you know what I mean."

"Whatever," I say, shaking my head. I hand the joint back to him. "Look, I don't smoke the stuff."

"It's no different than drinking a beer, except less calories," he says, grinning. "C'mon."

"I don't feel right about this."

"Are you kidding me? You grow the stuff."

"So what? Lots of farmers in the area used to grow tobacco, but they didn't necessarily smoke cigarettes. It's a crop. And I don't have to eat broccoli just because I grow it."

Ferg slides the entire joint into his mouth and gently pulls it out.

"Why did you do that?"

"I'm wetting it so it doesn't burn too fast."

"Where did you learn that?" I ask with raised eyebrows.

"At Delhi District Secondary School."

"Fergus Becker, are you telling me you did drugs in high school?" I ask, not even bothering to hide my surprise.

"That's what I'm telling you," he says while burning the end of the joint with a lighter. "Now are you going to join me? You know you want to try it." Ferg holds the end of the joint up to his lips with his thumb and index finger and inhales, holding it in his lungs. He stretches his hand with the joint out toward me and exhales.

"I don't know."

"C'mon."

I take it from him, hold it up to my lips, and draw in air. My lungs fill with smoke, and I immediately break into a coughing fit.

"Don't inhale so much smoke, and try to hold it in," Ferg instructs, slapping my back.

After a minute, I stop coughing. My throat feels raw, but I try to inhale again. I draw in a little bit of smoke. My lungs hurt, and I'm forced to exhale in less than ten seconds. The coughing fit returns.

Ferg laughs. "You are pathetic." He grabs the joint from me and takes a big, long draw. While he's holding it in, he hands it back and I try it again, this time with more success. After a couple of minutes, it's burned down to a nub. Ferg lowers the window and tosses it out of the car.

"I don't feel anything."

"That must be what every rookie says. You will," says Ferg as he shifts the cruiser into drive and hits the gas.

"Where are we going?"

"To the all-night diner for something to eat."

"Wait. You can't drive stoned."

"Sure, I can."

"This evening is going from bad to worse," I say, pulling out my phone.

"What are you doing?"

"I'm calling Meryl."

"Seriously? What are you going to tell her? You got high and now we're driving around town?" asks Ferg. "Put that away."

He's right, so I slip it back into my pocket. A warm, euphoric feeling spreads through me, and the last thing I want to do under this condition is talk to my wife. A gnawing sensation fills my stomach, so a trip to the diner seems more appealing now.

Up ahead, there's a slow-moving car that we're quickly approaching. "Look at this guy driving like my ninety-year-old granny," says Ferg, as he proceeds to pass to the left. "He's also got a taillight out."

"Ain't that Des' car?"

"I believe you are correct," he says, turning on his emergency flashers.

"What the fuck are you doing?" I ask as the euphoria is replaced with paranoia. "We can't have him see us like this."

"We're doing fine, but he won't be."

Desmond pulls his car over to the side of the road and comes to a stop.

I grab Ferg's arm before he steps out of the car. "Forget about him. Let's head straight to the diner. I'm starving."

"The diner can wait. It's open all night."

He pulls his arm free away and slides out of the cruiser. I dive across the front seat and try to stop him, but he's already slipped out. My head is spinning, but I decide I better stop him before he does something crazy, so I scramble out of the car. As we approach, Desmond rolls down his window.

Desmond scowls once he recognizes us. "If it isn't Batman and Robin, Delhi's famous crime-fighting duo."

"It's good to see you too, Des. Do you know that one of your rear lights is out?"

"No, but thanks for pointing it out. I'll have it looked at in the morning."

"Hang on there," responds Ferg. "That's an offense under section sixty-two of the Highway Traffic Act. I'm going to have to give you a ticket."

"Are you kidding?" asks Desmond, his face turns a deep shade of red.

"I'm deadly serious."

I find Ferg's response amusing. I try to suppress a laugh but finally burst out laughing. The more I try to stop, the harder I laugh.

"What the hell is so funny?" asks the mayor.

By now I'm sprawled on the ground howling. Ferg ignores me while he writes up the ticket.

"Is he drunk?" asks Desmond.

"No, just happy to see you," he says, handing him the ticket. "You make sure you get that light replaced. Have a good night."

"Fuck you, Becker."

Ferg grabs my arm and pulls me off the ground. "Let's go, buddy, and drag our asses to that diner."

Staggering back to the cruiser, I catch my breath. "Did you see the look on Des' face?" I ask, still giggling. "Man, he looked pissed."

Ferg breaks up laughing and slaps me on the back. "How about we finally get those greasy burgers?"

"Sure thing, but no more traffic stops. I've had enough excitement for one night."

CHAPTER 18

The following morning comes far too soon for my liking. Late nights are a thing of the past, and now I remember why. My head is pounding as I stumble into the kitchen. Meryl is emptying the dishwasher. I brush past her, mumble a greeting, and head straight to the carafe filled with coffee.

"I didn't hear you come in last night," she says, closing the dishwasher. "Did something happen in the greenhouse?"

"Greenhouse four was broken into," I mutter between gulps of coffee.

"Jesus Murphy! Was there much damage? Did we lose product?"

I slide down into a chair by the table. "It wasn't too bad. We lost some plants. Looked like a smash and grab type of thing. I called Ferg to take a look."

"You look pretty rough. What time did you get in?"

"Late. We ended up at the diner for some grub."

"And I suppose you two were drinking."

"No...we were, umm, smoking some weed."

"You've got to be kidding!" she shouts, slapping the back of my head with her hand.

"Hey!" Her voice and the impact of the blow reverberate in my skull. I grab hold of the table to keep from falling over. "What was that for?"

"Because the two of you act like little kids. So, you might as well be treated like one."

"Remember, it's legal now."

"It's not exactly legal to be driving around at night stoned," she mutters, shaking her head. "I suppose the mess in greenhouse four hasn't been cleaned up yet."

"Ferg told me not to touch it. He's going to send someone over today to check for evidence. I better get moving and make sure no one goes into the greenhouse."

When I finally step outside, the sun has climbed well above the horizon, scorching everything in its way. Bess is hiding in the shelter we built next to the house. I drive to the greenhouses and find an empty police squad car. I poke my head inside greenhouse four and recognize Nadine Stutz and Bruce Greening. They've been on the force for less than three years. Nadine is average height for a woman with a stocky build and broad shoulders. She looks like she could take down most guys without any help. Bruce is not what you would consider buff, more like Ferg's build. He's got his top shirt button undone and his tie is lopsided.

"Morning, Bruce, Nadine." I say, with a nod of my head.

"How's it goin', eh?" says Bruce.

"Pretty good. Except for this crap."

"You got yourself a real mess here," says Nadine.

"Yeah, plan to clean up once you're done here," I say. "Have you come up with anything useful?"

"There are prints on the door, but right now we ain't sure if they're from your robbers or people working on the farm. Also, there are two partial boot prints in some of the spilt soil. There are no tire prints because the ground is dried up and hard."

"We learnt all this in police school," says Bruce.

"You don't say," I reply. "I guess you don't have much to go on then."

"Ferg says you got security video," says Nadine. "That might tell us more than any prints we find here."

"Oh, yeah. I forgot about that. Follow me to the house, and I'll give you the tape."

CHAPTER 19

Although it's still morning, the heat and the humidity are already unbearable. I pull out the sponge from the bucket of soapy water and scrub the roof of our SUV, then slowly work my way down to the front windshield and hood. Tossing the sponge back into the bucket, I grab the hose and rinse off the vehicle before the soapy film dries.

While stopping to wipe my brow, a van slowly drives toward the house. When it gets closer, I realize it's a TV news van from CLCL in London. As the driver parks next to me, he and the passenger hop out.

"How can I help you folks?" I ask, looking warily at the visitors.

The passenger, a short blonde woman, in a black skirt with a red blazer, flashes a broad smile in my direction. "You must be Preston McPherson." I nod. "I'm Casey McBride, a reporter from CLCL news, and this is Harry, my cameraman."

"Nice meeting you both," I say. I'm not sure what to make of these two. "I suppose this is about my farm."

"Yes. Is it alright if we do a short interview?"

"I guess so," I say with a sigh.

"That's great," she says and turns to her colleague. "You can set up out here."

Harry pulls out a portable video camera and a tripod from the back of the van. I realize I look a mess. "Should I go inside to change?"

"No, you look fine," she says as she grabs a microphone from Harry. "I want to ask you a few questions about the picketers."

I lean forward thinking I didn't hear right. "Did you say picketers?"

"Yes. The ones out front."

"In front of my farm?"

"Yes. Didn't you know?"

Harry moves into position to film the interview. "Ready for a sound check, Casey."

I sprint to my half-washed car and hop in.

Casey runs after me. "Mr. McPherson, what about our interview?"

"It'll have to wait!" I yell as I peel down the driveway.

When I arrive at the farm entrance, I find a line of cars parked on the shoulder of the county sideroad. A scrum made up of thirteen women stands outside the entrance to the farm holding placards with Lucille Lamont in the middle. That Lucille is such a fucking pain in the ass. My first instinct is to run the bunch of them down with my car. I decide to stay calm. I pull out my phone to call our new security officer.

"Hello, Mr. McPherson."

"Habib, there's a group of women on the road in front of the farm."

"You want me to send them away?"

"I doubt they will leave but give it a try. Just make sure they don't step foot on the property. If they do, call the police and have them charged with trespassing."

"Very good, sir."

Nothing for me to do here. I head back to the house to speak to the news reporter.

***

"Ladies, it's going to be quite a hot day," says Lucille, mopping her forehead with a handkerchief. "Make sure you drink enough. I've brought cases of water, so help yourself."

One woman pushes through to the front. "I've brought lots of sunscreen for anyone who needs it."

"Thank you, Ida," says Lucille. "And thank you, Anne Marie, for printing these wonderful signs. Everyone, aren't they lovely?"

The group responds with applause.

"Anne Marie, I particularly like the sign that says *Be A Good Deeder Not A Weeder*," someone yells. "It's very clever."

"Indeed. Now, let me go over what we have planned for this afternoon," says Lucille. "If anyone attempts to enter the farm, we will block their way. The objective is to disrupt the operation as much as possible."

"What if no one tries to drive in?" asks a woman with a yellow and pink sundress and a large floppy straw hat with a pink bowknot.

"Well...umm," says Lucille, her forehead in a frown. "It's no big deal. We're going to be picketing in front of the farm entrance with our signs and anyone driving by will see them."

That prompts the group to raise their signs and wave them in the air.

"I've also designed a brochure on the dangers of marijuana that I've distributed every Sunday at church. If anyone driving by happens to stop, we can hand them a brochure." Lucille claps her hands. "Let's go, ladies. Start picketing!"

The women form a line and march back and forth in front of the road leading to the farm. Each time a car drives past, they wildly wave their signs. About fifteen minutes into the picketing, the CLCL news van returns to the roadway. The picketers mob the van as it parks on the shoulder. Casey lowers her window. "Which one of you is Mrs. Lamont?"

Lucille nudges past the others. "I am," she says with a look of superiority.

"I'm Casey McBride, and we would like to do a news story on your protest. Is it alright to film you walking in front of the farm and then interview one or two of you?"

"Certainly," she bellows and then turns to address her group. "Everyone get back in formation. We're going to be on TV."

Shortly after the news crew depart, the summer heat begins to drain the enthusiasm out of the band of protesters.

A tall woman wearing lime green slacks and a white t-shirt stops marching and approaches Lucille. "I don't know how much longer I can do this. I tired and my feet hurt."

"It's your shoes, Edna," says Lucille, looking down at her feet. "You should have brought flat shoes for walking. Why would you wear heels?"

"Because they match what I'm wearing. My sneakers are red."

"Why don't you drive home and change your shoes?"

"I need to pick up Gayle from her play date in an hour. There's no point in going home and coming back. I'll wear better footwear at the next protest."

"Very well," says Lucille with a deep sigh. "We'll carry on without you."

Edna staggers over to her car and drives off. The picketers resume parading back and forth.

Several minutes later, a silver Ford Escort approaches from the farm-side of the roadway. The car stops at the entrance and a dark-skinned man in a blue security guard uniform steps out of the vehicle.

"What do you think you're doing?" he shouts, leaning against the barrier gate.

Lucille steps forward. "What does it look like we're doing? We're conducting a protest in front of this sinful business."

The security guard scratches the day-old stubble on his chin, trying to decide what to make of the group. "Umm, this is private property," he says, pointing to a *No Trespassing* sign.

"Who are you?" asks Lucille, putting down her sign and leaning on the wooden stake.

"I am Habib, Mr. McPherson's security officer."

"Is that so?" asks Lucille, lowering her head to study him. "How long have you been employed at this immoral enterprise?"

"Madame, I have been working here for five days. Please do not cause me trouble."

The women stop parading and crowd behind Lucille. Someone yells out, "You can't stop us! We aren't on the property."

"No, no, no," he says, waving his arms. "You cannot be here."

Lucille takes a step forward. "How are you going to stop us?"

A gun blast thunders across the farm, startling the women. Habib ducks behind his car.

From behind a tree steps Preston's mother with a shotgun trained on the group. "Now what do we have here?" she asks. "Looks like a lynching to me."

"What are you talking about? This is preposterous," says Lucille as she cautiously takes a step forward. "Mrs. McPherson, put that gun down before someone gets hurt."

"Hold it right there or I shoot your ugly head off!" she hollers, taking aim for Lucille's neatly coiffed head.

Lucille scurries back to the group. "Good Lord, someone do something."

"Don't worry, Lucille, I've called the police," says Anne Marie.

Lucille shouts back to Mrs. McPherson from the back of the group. "You hear that? I hope they lock you up. I hope they lock up your entire family."

Preston's mother creeps over to Habib who is still cowering at the rear of his car. "Are you alright, boy?" she asks, walking back to have a look at who's behind the vehicle. "Come on out from there."

"Madame, please do not shoot me."

"I'm not going to shoot you," she says. "Are you one of those runaway slaves?"

"What are you talking about?" he asks, brushing the dirt from his uniform. "I am an engineer from Lebanon. This is the only job I could find in Canada."

A police cruiser races down the road toward the farm. At the last moment, the driver jams on the brakes and pulls the vehicle up behind the other cars parked at the side of the road. The driver's door flings open and out of the cruiser pops Ferg. He saunters toward the crowd gathered in front of the farm.

"What the heck is going on here?"

Everyone responds at once, screaming their version of the events. "Hold it!" shouts Ferg, throwing his arms up in the air. He points to Habib. "What's your story?"

"I'm the new security officer at the farm. I came down to the road to investigate a disturbance."

"Mac hired security?"

"Yes, sir."

"Awesome." Ferg spins around to face the group of ladies. "Which of you is the ringleader?"

"I organized this protest if that's what you're asking," says Lucille, stepping forward from the scrum with her chest puffed out.

"I should have known," says Ferg, shaking his head. "Why are you harassing these nice people?"

"You know very well what we are doing here. And you also know we have a right to express our views."

"Do you want me to take you in for disturbing the peace?"

"Me? That wretched woman fired a gun at us," says Lucille, pointing at Preston's mother. "That's who you should be arresting."

Ferg lumbers over to her and pulls the gun from her hands. "What are you doing firing a shotgun at people?"

"I thought they were lynching this poor black boy," she says defiantly.

"He's not black or a boy," he says. "Habib, why don't you take Mrs. McPherson back to the house."

Lucille charges toward Ferg. "You're going to let her go? She tried to kill us."

"That's right," he says, pulling his cap down over his forehead. "I'm letting all of you looney toons go. So, clear out. The party is over."

"We might as well," says one woman. "I need to get home to make Harold dinner."

"I've got to pick up Mandy from the daycare."

"I've got a headache. I need to go home and lie down."

"Very well," declares Lucille. "But we'll be back!"

The women stroll back to their cars. Anne Marie collects the signs and piles them into the back of her white Chevrolet Suburban. One by one, they drive off, leaving only Ferg by the side of the road.

"That's enough excitement for one day," grumbles Ferg, wiping the sweat from his brow with his arm. He places Mum's shotgun in the trunk of his cruiser and hops inside, cranking up the air conditioning. The cruiser crawls toward the farmhouse, kicking up clouds of dust. In the past, the fields would be full of stalks of corn, spreading out in the summer sun, but now they're dormant acres of dirt with patches of thistle with its spiny leaves and purple flowers.

***

Ferg drags himself out of the car and removes the gun from the trunk. He shuffles into the house where he finds me having lunch.

I look up and smile. "I heard from Habib that there was a ruckus out front involving Mum."

Ferg carefully places the shotgun on the table and pulls up a chair. "Yeah, Mum tried to blow Lucille's head off."

"That's what happens when you hold roadside Bible study classes," I say, smirking.

"This is no joke. I'm sure Desmond is going to complain to my superintendent. You need to keep the guns out of her reach."

"But pulling him over to hand him that ticket was fine. What did your superintendent say about that?"

"He wasn't too happy about that."

"No kidding."

"How's the security guy working out?"

"He's okay. Bright enough fellow, but not very intimidating."

"By the way, did you hear from Nadine?" asks Ferg.

"I did. She mentioned that the images from our security cameras were poor."

"Yeah, two guys involved were dressed in black and wore masks. We can't make out the make of the vehicle or plates."

"So, I guess that's the end of this?"

"The file will remain open," says Ferg. "But without more clues, this isn't going to get solved any time soon."

Meryl walks in the room carrying a vacuum cleaner. "Hey, Ferg. I thought I heard you."

"Now that I have you both here," says Ferg, "there is something I would like to talk to you about."

Meryl puts down the vacuum looks across the room with a wrinkled brow. "What is it now?"

"The night of the greenhouse break-in, Mac and I were discussing possibly replacing some of the lost revenue by selling some cannabis to American buyers."

"You mean the night you two got stoned and went joy riding in your police cruiser?"

"You told her?"

I shrugged. "Ferg, I told you I'm not interested."

"You're not interested in one hundred grand?"

"Where did you come up with that figure?" I ask, leaning forward in my chair. "You originally said I would only sell forty pounds of weed."

"That's right. Ramone is paying in U.S. funds, which works out to close to one hundred thousand dollars. All in cash."

Damn it; but it does sound enticing. A one-time sale can replace the money lost in the break-in and provide some desperately needed cash flow. "Who is this Ramone?"

"Mac!" shouts Meryl. "You better not be considering this."

"I'm just hearing him out."

"I can hear those wheels turning in your head. I know how this goes. First you say no to his off-the-wall proposal. Then he goes on a charm offensive and chips away at you. He'll tell you nothing will go wrong. This guy is an honest legit businessman. Sure, you're breaking the law, but no one cares." She turns and glares at Ferg. "We've heard it all before."

"And explain how we get the cannabis to this Ramone person?" I ask.

"Mac!"

"Meryl, let's hear him out."

"Ramone is a distributer in Michigan -"

"You mean a drug dealer," says Meryl, glowering with her arms crossed.

"He normally buys from local grey market producers -"

"You mean illegal grow-ops."

"Ramone typically pays cash for his product because -"

"He's also into money laundering, which happens to be a federal offense," Meryl interrupts, shooting daggers at Ferg.

"You don't have to worry about delivering the product because Ramone will arrange to pick it up and transport it over the border by -"

"You mean smuggle it over the border."

"Meryl, stop interrupting and let him finish," I say, throwing my arms in the air.

"We're tight on cash flow but we can get by without dirtying ourselves like this," pleads Meryl.

"Look Meryl, we are always *just getting by*," I say. "But we could use this infusion of cash. We've always made decisions together. Can't you back me on this one?"

"He will bring it over the border, so there's no risk to you," says Ferg. "By the way, he has other clients in Canada. This is a sound business model."

Mum traipses into the room in a bright yellow dress with a white purse and matching shoes. "Who is looking for a model? You know I once caught the eye of numerous hunky men."

I shake my head in frustration. "Mum, we need to chat about you and guns but now is not a good time."

"Fine. I know when I'm not wanted." She scoots out of the kitchen and into the living room.

"I'll go along with the arrangement," says Meryl, pointing a finger at me. "But it's going to only happen this one time. Understood?"

Both Ferg and I nod.

"But if you get caught, I hope you enjoy the jail time," Meryl says as she storms out of the room.

"Did I hear jail time?" Mum calls out from the living room. "We're talking about modeling, not hooking."

CHAPTER 20

The line of cars on the Ambassador Bridge snakes down onto Highway 3 in Windsor. I check the wait time on my phone app. "It's going to be a good forty minutes."

I glance over to Ferg, who has one hand on the steering wheel and the other on a cup of coffee. "We got lots of time," he says, taking a sip. "Do you mind passing my bagel over to me?"

"How? Do you have a third hand I don't know about, or do you plan to steer with your knees?"

"Steer with my knees, of course. We're barely moving."

"I hope you know where you're going. I don't want to end up in the wrong part of Detroit and have you pull out your service revolver."

Ferg spills coffee on his lap, which causes him to drop the bagel. "Ouch!" He grabs a napkin to sop up the coffee on his pants. "Don't worry, that's not going to happen. I can't bring a gun over the border."

"Thank God for small miracles."

"Look two rows over - the cars are moving better than in this one."

"Don't bother to -"

Before I can finish my thought, Ferg pushes his way into the other lane. He flashes his police badge out the driver side window. The other drivers don't seem too impressed and flip him the bird. I sink into my seat to avoid eye contact with anyone.

It takes another twenty-five minutes until we finally reach the front of the line. As our car rolls up to the booth, Ferg turns to me. "Let me do all the talking."

"Seriously, I'd like to know how to get you to stop talking for once."

"Screw you, Mac," he says, grinning. Ferg rolls down his window and hands the border agent our passports.

"Nationality?"

"We're both Canadian," says Ferg.

"Can't he talk?" asks the agent, almost growling.

"Yes, I can. I'm also Canadian."

"Where do you both live?"

"Norfolk County," says Ferg.

The border agent glares at me.

"Norfolk County, as well."

"What type of work do you do?"

"I'm a police sergeant with the Ontario Provincial Police."

"I'm a farmer."

"What do you grow?"

Ferg looks at me out of the corner of his eyes, subtly shaking his head, reminding me that I can't say I grow marijuana or I'll be denied entry into the U.S. "I'm a dairy farmer."

Maybe I'm imagining it, but I could swear he snickered. And rolled his eyes. Another city person looking down at farming, like it's a profession for dimwitted people. *Where does he think his food comes from?*

I strain my neck toward the open driver-side window. "You know that agriculture is the backbone of this country. Farmers put up with random weather, lurking pestilence, and pollution to protect our land and ensure that Canadians have fresh, safe, and healthy produce to eat. We have been the economic engine of this country since before Confederation!"

The agent glances down at us, his eyes blinking. "What's with him?" he asks Ferg.

"Oh, he's always like this. We ignore him."

The agent turns away from our car to slide our passports through his computer. When he's done, he returns them. "What is the purpose of your visit?"

"We're going for lunch," responds Ferg.

The agent lowers his gaze, furrowing his eyebrows. "You've come all this way just for lunch?"

"Absolutely! I have a craving for ribs at Bobby's Barbeque," responds Ferg. I think he was smacking his lips. I hope he doesn't drool on the border agent.

"Are you bringing over any firearms, food products, tobacco products, alcohol or animal products?"

"No," I respond.

"Are either of you employed in the Canadian cannabis industry?"

I swallow hard and force a smile. "No."

"Okay, enjoy your lunch."

As we pull away from the booth, I exhale.

"That was a piece of cake, Mac."

"I can't believe he asked if I grew weed. Do you think he believed me?"

"He didn't actually ask if you grew weed. That was a standard set of questions they ask, so relax."

Ferg turns onto a ramp for Interstate 75. The car accelerates, and he merges into traffic on the highway. "How long will it take to reach the meeting place?" I ask.

"Not long, but we're stopping for ribs at Bobby's."

"I thought you made that up."

"When it comes to food, I'm always serious."

"I want to get this meeting over with and then blow out of town."

"Asshole!" Ferg leans on the horn when another driver cuts into his lane. "It's lunch time and we gotta eat, right?"

"I suppose."

"I promise, it'll be worth the drive. It's not that much out of the way."

Ferg exits the highway onto Seven Mile Road. When we stop at a light, a black kid on the curb with red high-top basketball shoes is watching us. He has a baseball bat in his hands. No ball or glove. I check that the doors are locked. The kid smirks, a subtle white slash of a smile, eyes dark. The light turns green, and I exhale. Inexpressive bodies wander onto the road without looking, giving us the finger as we drive past.

Ferg has filled me in on Ramone Lopez. His parents are immigrants and settled in Mexicantown, which is not far from downtown and the Ambassador Bridge. Ramone's parents operate a Mexican grocery store. Ferg describes Ramone as an entrepreneur who began selling marijuana as a teen well before Michigan decriminalized it. As Ferg puts it, "he hasn't transitioned his business to a state-licensed enterprise." Despite not owning a criminal record, my hunch is that Ramone doesn't quite fit the profile that the state is looking for.

"I'm not getting a good feeling out here," I say, grimacing. "Are you sure this is safe?"

"It's fine out here. You don't see any rusted-out cars or boarded up homes?"

I study the scene outside the car. Maybe it's not too bad. When we turn off, we drive down a road with a lot of churches. Not the type of churches I'm familiar with back home. These are small, single-storey, red brick buildings with names like Ministry of Deliverance and Church of the Good People. The only other prevalent establishments are strip clubs. I suppose there's a convenience factor working here. First you indulge in sin and then seek forgiveness.

Ferg parks the car and shuts off the engine. "Here we are."

"Where?" I look around and, at first, only see another storefront church. There is a tiny, white-painted brick building next to it. There's no signage, only a hand-painted picture of barbequed ribs above the entrance and a red 'OPEN' neon sign in the window. Ferg hops out of the car. I reluctantly follow.

Inside, a faded sign states that Bobby's has been in business since 1984. The décor looks even older. Pedestal tables with chipped brown Formica tops are scattered around the restaurant along with mismatching chairs.

As we walk to the back of the restaurant, I give Ferg a nudge. "The windows are so filthy, that hardly any sunlight manages to filter through."

"We're not here for the décor."

"That's for sure."

I stop to look at the signed photos hanging on the walls of 'celebrities' that have visited the establishment. None of the names are familiar to me. What does stand out is the incredible aroma of smoked meat that hits me even before I walk in the door. "They have a Southern Pride smoker here which, in my books, is one of the best on the market," Ferg explains, pointing to the massive stainless-steel appliance behind the counter.

"Means nothing to me. But doesn't it get smoky in here?"

"Southern Pride uses gas, not wood. You can't have an indoor wood-burning smoker."

"So, why don't they get one for outside?"

"This is Michigan, not Texas."

Most of the tables are occupied, but I sit down at a table in the back. "It's cafeteria service so you hold the table and I'll order the food."

He walks to the counter, and I follow anyway. The girl behind the counter is wearing a white stained apron and disposable gloves. She smiles as we approach. "What can I get you guys?"

Before I can absorb the menu on the wall, Ferg is already blurting out our order.

"Your order will be ready in a couple of minutes," she says. "Your order number is thirty-two. Your total comes to $27.32."

"I got this," says Ferg.

"So, y'all from Canada?" asks the server.

"Yup," I say.

"We get a lotta Canadians coming in here. Though I never been to Canada. Don't have no passport," she says. "Do you guys know Drake? He's from Canada, right?"

"Yeah, he's Canadian," I say. "Don't know him personally."

"Drake is the only thing I know about Canada. Oh, and the Raptors."

Ferg pulls on my arm. "Let's grab a table before they fill up."

We hustle to back to our table. I grab a napkin and brush the crumbs off my seat before sitting down. As I gaze around the restaurant, it strikes me that we're the only white faces in the place. I lower my gaze to Ferg, sitting opposite me.

About ten minutes later, the girl behind the counter calls out our order. "Thirty-two is ready for pickup."

When we are done eating, I check the time on my phone. "How far is the meeting place from here?"

"Can't be more than fifteen minutes."

"Then we need to finish here in the next ten minutes."

"Stop stressing. We'll be fine."

I reach into a pocket for a bottle of antacid tablets to settle my jumpy stomach. "I just want this day to be over. I have a bad feeling about this business."

"You are such a worrier." Ferg reaches across the table to pick up the plate that had the onion rings. "Do you want the last one?"

"Go ahead."

"More for me!"

As we pile back into the car, the heavy meal is already making me sleepy. The neighbourhoods we pass through look progressively worse. An object bounces off our hood, startling me. My head swivels around.

"Relax, that was only some kids playing stick ball," says Ferg.

"How much farther?"

"It should be the next block."

The car comes to a stop in front of Jiggy's Bar. The windows and front door have security bars. This place makes Bobby's Barbeque look like a five-star establishment. Is it possible to get a negative star rating?

Ferg turns to me as he turns off the car. "Just stay relaxed and listen to what the man has to say."

"Is it safe to leave the car parked on this street?"

"It's broad daylight. Stop worrying."

We get out of the car and walk into the bar. It's dark and the place has a sour smell. There are a few guys sitting at the bar alone, drinking draft beer. Ferg walks up to the bartender, who is chatting with one of the customers. "Excuse me, we're looking for Ramone."

The bartender looks us up and down. "Do I look like a goddam secretary?"

"He told us to meet him here," responds Ferg.

"He's in the back, playing pool."

We walk in the direction of the backroom but, before we reach the door, a tough-looking, young black guy in low-rise jeans and a white sleeveless undershirt steps in front of us. He has tattoos covering his arms, chest, and face. "Where y'all think you're goin'?"

"We're here to see Ramone," says Ferg.

He turns his head toward the pool room, "Hey Ramone. You expectin' two white dudes?"

"Yeah, let them in," a voice replies from inside the room.

I try to walk through the door when an arm comes up and stops me from going forward. "Hang on there," he says. "I gotta make sure you ain't carryin' no pieces."

Ferg raises his arms to above his shoulders, and I follow his lead. I wonder if he notices how much I'm shaking. I want to turn around and run back to the car. My lunch is about to come back up as his hands pat me down. After being frisked, we are allowed in.

There are four pool tables in the room but only one is being used. Two guys hold pool cues in their hands while five others stand around the table watching. One of the men puts his cue stick down and walks towards us. "Which one of y'all is Ferg?" he asks.

"That's me."

Ramone breaks out in a wide grin, displaying his gold teeth grill. Based on his appearance I can understand why the state would not be eager to provide him with a license. "Damn, only in Canada would you have a cop dealing."

"Hey, I'm just making introductions," says Ferg. "I'm not involved in the business."

Ramone turns and looks me over. "So, you must be the farmer dude."

"Umm, yeah. I'm Preston."

He shakes his head, grinning. "You don't look like the type to be running a grow-op."

"I run a legal and respectable farm. I'll have you know that agriculture is the backbone of our country. Farmers put up with random weather, lurking pestilence -"

"Pestilence," repeats one of the other men. "Why are you quoting the scriptures?"

"That's not from the scriptures," I say. "I'm trying to explain that as a farmer, I have a duty to ensure that Canadians have fresh, safe, and healthy produce to eat and -"

"I thought y'all growing weed," says Ramone, his face contorts as he looks over to Ferg.

"He does grow weed," says Ferg. "Mac, shut the fuck up. You're confusing everyone with your farmer sermon."

One of the other men walks over to us. "Can I ask you something?"

"Umm, sure," I say.

"Do you know Drake?"

"No, we don't know Drake," I say.

"This here is my associate, Angel." Ramone directs us to a booth in the corner. "Have a seat so we can talk. Angel, bring these boys something to drink."

"I'll have a Stroh's," says Ferg.

"A pop would be fine for me," I say.

"Bring the man a pop," says Ramone, snickering and rolling his eyes. "So, what type of weed are you growing up there in Canada?"

"I've got Purple Dream, some Sour Diesel and Blue Dawg for now," I say.

Ramone nods his head. "That's some good shit."

Angel returns with drinks and slides into the booth next to Ramone.

"If the quality is good," says Ramone, between sips of beer, "I'm paying nineteen hundred a pound."

Jesus Murphy, that's twenty-five hundred in Canadian dollars. A thousand more than I'm currently getting. "That sounds reasonable." My eyes are just about popping out of my head.

"I will be looking to buy fifty pounds a month."

"I'm only looking to sell forty pounds."

"Forty pounds a month?"

"No, just forty pounds."

Ramone glares at Ferg. "Why the fuck y'all wastin' my time?"

"Hang on, hang on," says Ferg as he grabs me by the arm and pulls me away from the table. Ferg shoves his face into mine. "What the fuck are you doing?"

"Remember, I only want to replace the lost revenue from the robbery."

"You were complaining about the low margins, right?"

"Yeah."

"This is your chance to make some decent money and keep the farm going."

I repeatedly stab him the chest with my index finger. "You want me to do business with drug dealers?"

"Ramone is an entrepreneur like you."

My head shakes vigorously in response. "He's not anything like me. He's got gold-plated braces and tattoos all over his body. Did you know that he was going to make me this offer and didn't bother to tell me?"

"I had no idea. I wouldn't do that to you. But fifty pounds a month is over one million dollars a year. Think about it. That can make a big difference in your life and your family."

"Sure, I can end up in jail."

"Just listen to what he has to say," says Ferg, putting his arm around my shoulders. "I'm sure you can work out something."

I hold my hands at my temples and let out a sigh. "Okay, okay, let's hear what he has to say."

We slide back into the booth. I have my elbows on the table and lean forward. "So, if I agree to sell you fifty pounds of weed each month, how am I get to get it over the border to you?"

"I'll arrange for a boat to cross Lake Erie at night to pick up each shipment on the Canadian side."

"We can scout out a secluded location where it won't raise any suspicion," says Ferg.

"I like the way you think, dude," says Ramone, grinning. "You sure you're a cop?"

I look across the table. Do I want to be doing business with these people? Like, what could go wrong? I could get caught and locked up in prison. The drug dealers could kill me and my family. I could lose the farm. It's stupid even being here. But this much money is hard to turn down. We've been struggling financially for so many years. We might finally be able to live comfortably.

"Okay, I'm willing to try this on a trial basis," I say, nodding my head. "If I'm not happy with the arrangement, I walk away."

Ramone leans back with his hands behind his head. A menacing grin spreads across his face. "Dude, everyone is happy doing business with Ramone."

CHAPTER 21

I'm experiencing the jitters over the first marijuana delivery for Ramone. What if something goes wrong? What if he's not where he's supposed to be? Or someone sees us? Why do I let Ferg talk me into these things? *Because I'm fucking greedy.*

I toss the second bag of marijuana into the back of our SUV and check the time again. In the darkness, I make out the headlights of a vehicle driving toward the greenhouses. I can tell it's not Habib's car. Where is Habib?

As the vehicle gets closer, I recognize it. A police cruiser stops next to me, and Ferg bounces out from behind the wheel.

"What are you doing up so late?" I ask.

"I thought you could use some company."

"It's not much of a drive down to the Port Rowan Marina."

"Come on, Mac, you shouldn't be doing this alone."

"I'll be fine."

Ferg lowers his head, frowning. "I know, but it wouldn't hurt to have some company and backup in case something goes wrong. Not that anything *will* go wrong. Like you said, it'll be fine."

I slam the hatch shut. "Do you ever actually listen to what you say? Sure thing, hop in." I slip behind the wheel while Ferg gets in next to me. Turning around in my seat, I reach down and pick up my shotgun. "Besides, I already got some company."

"We better not need that thing," says Ferg shaking his head.

I slowly follow the gravel trail out the main entrance onto the main road. It's a moonless night and no other cars are on the road. Our headlights are the only thing that breaks up the blackness. Only after we turn onto Regional Road 16 do we pass the occasional car.

Out of the corner of my eye, I catch Ferg yawning. "I hope you aren't on duty tomorrow. I don't want to be held responsible for you falling asleep at your desk," I say, smirking.

"Yeah, yeah. So, have you worked out how you can explain the fifty pound of product disappearing from the inventory every month?" asks Ferg.

I shrug. "We run a shoddy operation."

"Seriously."

"We're fine for this month. As I told Ramone, this is on a trial basis, so as far as I'm concerned, this will be our one and only shipment to him."

"You seem pretty calm about this. What have you got up your sleeve?"

"I've got a couple of ideas. Maybe I'll grow a few plants away from the greenhouses. Or there could be a sudden drop in the size of the buds in the next month."

He slaps me on arm and lets out a cackle. "You're starting to think like me."

A light rain begins to fall, and I turn on the wipers. It's over a half hour drive to the marina, which means we'll be there shortly after midnight. Both the town and marina are closed at this hour. When we reach Lakeshore Drive, I can make out the lake on our left - a black void that stretches across the horizon. We pass by closed gas stations, fast food restaurants, and gift shops. I turn left onto Dock Street and continue until the road ends at the lake. Peering across the unlit pier, I try to pick out where our contacts might be waiting. On the outer side of the dock, there's a berth with a boat that has its lights on. The reflections of the illuminated craft shimmer on the water's surface.

I get out of the car and open the back hatch. Ferg grabs one of the bags, and I pull out the other. The rain has slowed down to a light drizzle, but the dampness and cool breeze blowing off the lake makes me shiver. As we walk toward the moored boat, the only sound is the water lapping against the pier. I have the urge to turn around and drive home. Ferg's presence is the only thing that keeps me from bolting. We say nothing as we walk down the slippery pier toward the partially lit boat. As we approach, someone shines a flashlight torch in our faces.

"Is that you, McPherson?"

"Yeah, is that Ramone?"

"Dude, Ramone don't do no pickups."

When we reach the boat, I drop my bag onto the dock. From what I can make out in the dark, the boat is at least twenty-five feet long with dual outboard engines.

I now realize that it's Angel on the pier. He tosses the two bags of marijuana onto the boat deck. His companion opens the bags to examine the content. "Looks like good shit." He then seals the bags and stows them in a compartment behind the seats. Out of the same compartment, he pulls out a large brown envelope and tosses it onto the pier.

I shrug and look over at Ferg. He shakes his head. "What's that?"

Angel picks up the envelope and hands it to me, letting out a deep belly laugh. "That's your money for fuck's sake."

"It's in cash?"

"Yeah, we didn't have time to stop for a fucking bank draft," he says, climbing back into the boat. "We'll see y'all next month."

"Wait!" I shout out. "I never said there'd be another shipment."

Angel stiffens up and yanks a gun out of his waistband, pointing it at us. "Ramone will be expecting another delivery. He don't like to be disappointed."

Ferg is waiving his hands in the air. "Calm down. Ramone won't be disappointed."

Angel smirks at us and slips his gun back into his pants. He starts up the boat motor while his companion unties the line that's wrapped around a cleat on the pier. Once they're free, the boat slowly pulls away from the marina and disappears.

"Let's go, Mac," says Ferg.

I'm shaking as I hold the envelope tightly against my chest. "You fucking idiot!" I scream, not caring if someone hears us. "Now what am I going to do? I can pull together fifty pounds of product, but not every month."

"Calm down. It's late. You'll think of something after a good night sleep."

We creep back to the car. "I doubt I'll be getting a good night sleep any time soon."

Once we get back into the car, I rip open the envelope and peek inside. "Oh shit, it's in U.S. currency."

Damn it. It always seems to be one step forward, two steps back. Why can't I ever get a break? I swear I must be jinxed. I toss the envelope onto the backseat and head home.

CHAPTER 22

"Mr. McPherson, you're next...Mr. McPherson."

The girl behind the counter looks at me, awaiting my response. I approach the counter and eke out a half smile. "Sorry, Darlene. I had a late night."

"Gotcha. A coffee will wake you up. So, the usual, medium coffee?"

I nod. "And throw in a breakfast sandwich."

"That will be $5.42."

I pull out a bill out of my pocket and throw it on the counter. Darlene picks it up and examines it. "I'm sorry, Mr. McPherson, but I don't have change for a U.S. hundred-dollar bill. Do you have anything smaller?"

I take back the bill and stuff it back into my pocket. "Oh, sorry. I was in Detroit recently and still have some American cash in my pocket." I take out my wallet and hand her my debit card.

"Your order will be ready in a few minutes. Have a great day."

"Thanks." I step over to the pickup counter with a hand in my pocket, fingering the one-hundred-dollar bill. Now that was dumb, pulling out a big bill in Tim Hortons. Hardly what I would call discreet. Someone drops off my order at the counter. I grab it and plop down at an empty table.

I unwrap the sandwich and take a few bites. I'm not hungry, only tired and confused. I'm about to take a sip of coffee when I hear someone calling my name. "Hey, Mac. Are you there?"

I look up and see Ferg sitting opposite me. "Hey, when did you get here?"

"I've been sitting in this seat for at least the last minute waiting for you to notice," says Ferg. "You're, like, lost in space."

I wrap my sandwich back up. "Sorry, I'm tired. I don't think I even got two hours sleep."

"Are you not going to eat that?"

I push it across the table. "It's yours. How is it that you don't look the least bit tired?"

"Remember, I'm a cop. I'm used to working night shifts."

I lean forward and look around to check if anyone is paying attention to us. "What am I going to do with all that U.S. cash?" I say in a whisper.

"I guess we didn't quite think this all the way through."

"Handing out U.S. hundred-dollar bills all over town isn't going to raise too much suspicion," I say sarcastically with raised eyebrows.

"Yeah. Not a wise move. Got any ideas on what you're going to do?"

"Not really. Are you busy Thursday evening?"

"Nope. I'm off duty after five o'clock."

"Good. I think we need to call a family meeting and develop an action plan."

"Mac, you're telling Graham what you've been up to? He's going to go ape shit on us."

"Hell, no! I'm not inviting the entire McPherson clan. Today's topics are best kept within the immediate family." I get up to leave.

"Where are you going?" asks Ferg.

"I'm going home to talk to Meryl about this. I slipped out this morning without sharing all of the details."

"Good luck with that."

***

Habib sits in his vehicle, taking sips of sweet tea, and watching the line of placard-carrying women march back and forth in front of the entrance to the property. Some passing cars honk in approval. A few drivers slow down to display a one-finger salute.

When the women first began their protest in July, they were picketing once a week. The media coverage that followed brought out a lot more protesters. Many of the new people are not local but are motivated to join because they oppose cannabis legalization. The protests have spread to several days a week.

Lucille begins her pep talk. It's the same one she does at the start of each picketing session. "Thank you, everyone, for coming out today. This is an important cause, and I'm so pleased to see some new supporters out today. Please raise your hand if this is your first time."

Three people in the group raise a hand. Lucille claps her hands, and the rest of the group joins in. "Our protest is intended to remind the community of this sinful farm and to make life difficult for them. If anyone attempts to enter the property, we will link arms and block their way. There are refreshments in a cooler, compliments of Goodfellow's Market. Now let's get marching!"

Lucille leads the protesters, strutting around like a banty rooster and shouting encouragement. Habib shows up each day, watching from inside the property until they leave.

Over an hour passes before two white vans pull up and stop opposite the front gate. The drivers look puzzled as the women shout at them, waving signs. Phil Garneau lowers his window. "What's going on here?"

Lucille scampers over to his van. "This is a corrupt and evil enterprise. We are demanding that the government shut it down before our young are lured by their devilish offerings."

"I work for the federal government," he responds.

The delighted woman turns to face her flock. "Did you hear that, ladies? The government has finally showed up to shutter this place. Praise the Lord!"

"God has answered our prayers!" shouts Anne Marie as tears form in her eyes.

Habib climbs out of his vehicle to open the gate and clear the women out of the way. When the path is clear, the vans turn off the road and goes through the gate to the farmhouse up ahead.

***

Meryl is bent over the laptop in her office looking over spreadsheets. She takes a sip from her coffee mug in between pecking away on the keyboard as she enters the latest data. She hears someone at the front door and calls out, "Is that you, Mac?"

There's no answer, so she gets up from her desks and scrambles to the front door. When she swings the door open, the color from her face drains as she recognizes the two men standing on her porch.

"I'm Glen Fleming, an inspector from the Ontario Cannabis Agency."

"And I'm Phil Garneau, an inspector from the federal Department of Health."

They both hand Meryl their business cards, and Garneau reads the statement regarding government inspection policy and her legal rights.

"Yes, I...umm, remember you both," she says, stumbling over her words. "Are you here for an inspection?"

"Yes, we can start with the grow rooms," says Fleming.

"Let me call my husband. He had to run into town this morning."

Meryl pulls her phone from her pocket and pecks at the screen. "Hi, hon. I have two government inspectors at the house." She listens to his response. "Okay. I'll let them know."

She ends the call and puts down the phone. "He's on his way back and says to meet him at the greenhouses. I think you know the way."

"Thank you, Mrs. McPherson," replies Fleming. He turns toward his car and Garneau follows close behind.

***

After hitting the end button on my phone, I lean on the accelerator, causing the truck to shake as it rumbles down the road. As I pull up in front of the farm, I lean on the horn, startling the picketers marching outside the front gate. Habib opens the gate and I slowly move forward, forcing the protesters to move out of the way. As I drive into the property, I give Lucille a mocking wave and smile.

When I arrive at the greenhouses, the inspectors are inside their vans, waiting for me. As they exit their vehicles, I approach them. "How can I help you folks?"

"I'm Glen Fleming, an inspector from the Ontario Cannabis Agency."

"And I'm Phil Garneau, an inspector from the federal Department of Health."

"I know who you guys are," I say, forcing a smile.

They both hand me business cards, and Garneau starts to read his standard statement, but I interrupt him. "Guys, I've heard your spiel before. Can we just get to it?"

"We are required to advise you of our policies and your legal rights at each visit," says Garneau and he continues reading his lame statement.

Fleming walks toward the mother room. "We can start here."

"Sure. Sure," I say, walking ahead to open the door for them. "I didn't expect to see you guys so soon after the last inspection. You were here eight months ago."

Fleming stops and puts down the black case he's carrying. "We normally don't. Your last two reports showed a lot of destroyed plants. We're here to make sure there isn't a problem with your setup."

I've been playing around with our inventory. Many of the plants that have been sold to the Michigan dealers have been reported as diseased and destroyed, but not all of them. There's still a shortfall between our records and actual plants on the farm. Beads of sweat form on my head, and I force a smile. "You didn't have to drive all the way out here. You could have called, and I would have provided you with an explanation."

Garneau walks past me and pushes open the greenhouse door. "It's our job."

"Let me know what I can do to help you along."

"We're fine, thanks," he says, while slipping on a pair of booties.

Fleming opens their black case and pulls out some equipment. "When we're done, we'll meet you at the house to go over your records." He motions to his partner to check out the greenhouse next to the one we're in.

"Sounds like a plan," I say, pulling the door open. "I'll leave you guys to do your inspecting."

Once outside, I clench my fists and mutter to myself. "Shit. Shit. Shit."

"What's wrong, Mr. McPherson?"

I turn around and find Jake, gawking at me. "The shit's going to hit the fan, son."

"I don't know nothin' about that, Mr. McPherson."

"No, you wouldn't. Can you round up some of the other workers? We need to move some plants around. I'll be right back."

"Yeah, I can do that," he says, scratching his head. "Although, kinda seems odd."

"Just do it! I'm going to head to the house."

I march over to my truck and scramble inside. I shift into drive and lean on the accelerator. The vehicle lurches forward in a cloud of dust. At the house, I leap from the truck and dash inside, heading straight to my office. Plopping down into my chair, I reach for my computer's power button.

"What the hell is going on?" I turn around and see Meryl standing at the door with her hands resting on her hips. "Is there a problem?"

"There will be if I don't adjust our inventory."

"Your problem started when you decided to cruise to Detroit to meet up with a drug dealer," says Meryl, her voice rising. "If that wasn't bad enough, who knows how many laws you're breaking running drugs over the border through the marina. Should I go on?"

"Not now!" I scream. "I've got to get the inventory in order for those inspectors. Are you going to help or just give me grief?"

"You can't add plants to the inventory," she says, shaking her head. "They're going to notice the discrepancy if they're counting the plants."

"Maybe not," I say, tapping on the computer keyboard. "I'm going to get the boys to move some of the plants around so that they double count a bunch of plants."

"Mac, listen to yourself. They're going to see you. This is not going to end well."

"Those bean counters, or whatever they are, aren't gonna see anything." I finish what I'm doing and power off the computer. "Okay, I'm heading back."

I jump back into my truck and race back to the greenhouses. Jake has several workers waiting in front of greenhouse four where a tractor and a flat-bed trailer are parked.

Hopping out of the truck, I shout at the group. "I want you to grab twenty-six plants in greenhouse four and put them in greenhouse three. Then stand by because we're going to have to move them back. You're going to have to be discreet."

"How do you be discreet?" asks Jake. He's wearing his dopey look.

"Jesus Murphy. Make sure the inspectors don't see you. Now hustle while I keep them distracted."

I rush back to the mother room as the inspectors are pulling the door open. "Hey there, are you done in here already?" I ask.

"That's right," says Garneau. "Let's move on to the next greenhouse."

I step in front of them to block their way. "Hang on, I've got a couple of questions to ask."

"What about?"

"Umm, I wanted your opinion on whether I've developed spores on some of the plants in this room." I look out the corner of my eye to see the guys loading plants onto the trailer.

"We didn't see any problems," says Fleming as he tries to walk past me.

I grab his arm and lead him back inside. "This will only take a minute." I stop in front of a plant, pulling off a leaf and turn it around to show them the back. "Do you see any spores on the back on this leaf?"

Fleming bends down and examines it. "I don't see anything abnormal, Mr. McPherson."

"Really? How about this one?" I walk two rows over and turn over another leaf. "I think this one might be infected."

"These plants look fine. If you have concerns, send some samples into your lab for testing. We need to get back to our inspection."

I rush to the door while trying to think of a reason to keep them here. The door swings open behind me and I almost fall backwards. I turn my head and see that it's Jake again. "Jake, have you finished unpacking the supplies off the truck?" I ask as I try to motion with my eyes in the direction of greenhouse four.

Jake looks perplexed. "Umm, no sir. But we did move those things for you."

"Yes, that's what I meant. If you had finished moving them off the truck."

Garneau and Fleming have already left the greenhouse, and I rush outside to join them. "Why don't we move on to greenhouse three?"

"Sure. It doesn't really matter," says Fleming. "We're going to all the rooms today."

As we turn the corner and walk toward number three, the staff are sitting on the flat-bed trailer, which is parked in front of the greenhouse three. I let the inspectors walk past me and, behind their backs, signal to the staff with my arm to get their collective asses out of here. One of the workers hops onto the tractor and hauls the trailer and the co-conspirators away.

Once I've hustled the inspectors into greenhouse three, I scramble outside and pull out my phone to call Jake.

"Hey, Mr. McPherson. What do you want us to do now?"

"I want you to take the guys over to greenhouse five and remove twenty-six plants just like you did in greenhouse three. Head over to greenhouse four and replace the plants that you moved to three. Do you got that?"

"Yes, sir."

"When we're done here, I'm bringing the inspectors over to greenhouse four. I'll call you when it's safe and you can move the twenty-six plants from three to five."

"Sure thing. We'll move plants from three to four then five to four."

"No! First move five to four and then three to five."

"I'm writing this down, Mr. McPherson, so we don't mess up."

"Good. Text me when four is ready for the inspectors. And try to keep out of sight. I don't need to have them see you joyriding around the farm with a load of plants."

"Don't worry, Mr. McPherson. We got this."

I put away my phone, knowing the future of my farm is in the hands of an idiot. I rush back into the greenhouse to check on inspectors Frick and Frack. They're at the far end of the greenhouse which means they are likely about done. "Need any help with anything?" I call out.

"No, we're fine," Garneau answers, not even looking up from his tablet. "We'll be done here shortly."

Crap. They're moving too quickly.

"Do you guys want to stop and grab a coffee? There's a fresh pot in our staff room, and my wife baked some cranberry muffins this morning."

"It's okay," he responds. "We need to get through this."

I survey the greenhouse for something that might delay them. I spot the breaker switch for the electrical power panel. Trying to be inconspicuous, I shuffle over to the panel and turn off the power. "Hey, that can't be good," I call out, peering up at the ceiling.

"You better have that looked at," remarks Fleming. "You don't want to throw off the environment in the room."

I stare at the panel, trying to appear bewildered. "Umm, yeah I know. Do you guys know anything about this stuff? The guy who looks after these things for me is off today."

Fleming puts down his tablet and strolls over to the electrical panel. He stares at the equipment for several moments then reaches out and flips the main breaker switch. The lights and equipment turn back on. "It seems your main breaker was tripped. It might have been an electrical surge or maybe something more serious. I would have your guy look at this when he comes in again to make sure there isn't an electrical problem."

"Hey, thanks so much." I gaze down at my phone, looking for a text from Jake. Nothing.

"Phil, let's wrap up in here and move on to the next one," says Fleming, walking back to where he left his tablet.

"I've got this one row left to do."

Beads of sweat form on the back of my neck. I need to come up with another stall. I can see that they are done and starting to make their way back to the front of the greenhouse.

"Umm, did I...umm mention that Meryl baked muffins this morning? She makes the best muffins in Norfolk County. Just ask the people at our church."

"Yes, you did mention the muffins," says Fleming. "We're going to move on to the next greenhouse."

My phone pings and I pull it out of the back pocket of my jeans.

Mr. McP we is done with #4.

"Absolutely! Let me take you to greenhouse four."

We scoot over to the next greenhouse to continue the process. Once inside, I text Jake to move the same number of plants out of greenhouse three and transfer them to five. I was thinking we might pull this off when Garneau approaches me.

"I've got to go back to the last room. I've forgotten my case."

"No, no, no," I stammer. "You can't go back."

"I need to get my case."

"What I mean is...umm, you need to finish up here. I'll get it for you."

"Okay, thanks."

I dash out of the greenhouse and race back to number three. Out front, the guys are loading plants onto the flat-bed trailer. I run past them and locate Garneau's case. Tucking it under my arm, I sprint past my staff who have now stopped to watch me with mix of puzzlement and amusement. Out of breath, I stagger into greenhouse four still clutching the case.

"Here...it...is," I say, gasping for air. I extend my right hand, which is holding the case.

Garneau takes it from me, shaking his head. "There wasn't any urgency. You could have walked it over." He sets it down and returns to conducting the inventory.

Maybe the wild gallop to get the case was a slight over reaction on my part. I pull out my phone to text Jake. *How's the transfer to #5 coming along?*

About a minute later, Jake responds. *Riding over to 5 right now.*

I lean up against the greenhouse wall. The inspectors are unaware of the shenanigans taking place under their noses. We might pull this off. Though my stomach is still in knots. As they slowly return to the front of the greenhouse, still no message from Jake. My mind goes blank. I can't think of something to stall them.

"We're ready to move on to the next greenhouse," says Fleming as he pushes to door open. "Lead the way."

I stand there frozen. Beads of sweat quickly collect on the back of my neck.

"Is something wrong?" asks Garneau.

"Wrong? Umm, no...did you want to go to the next greenhouse?"

"That's what I said," says Fleming, with a pinched expression. "We don't have all day."

Now I'm shaking but trudge toward greenhouse five. As I turn the corner, I see the trailer loaded with plants in front of greenhouse five. I tumble backwards into the two inspectors.

"Hey, are you okay?" asks Fleming, as he looks down at me bent over on the ground.

"Oh, the pain," I gasp.

The two inspectors look at each other, not sure what to do. Fleming bends down. "What's wrong?"

"I'm not sure...maybe I'm having...a heart attack."

"Glen, maybe we should call an ambulance," says Garneau.

"Wait," I moan. "It might be a cramp."

I hear my phone go *ping* and slip it out of my pocket.

Done!

I slowly pick myself off the ground and brush myself off. "Yeah, it must have been a cramp. It seems to have passed."

"Are you sure?" asks Garneau. "Maybe you should go to the hospital to be checked out just to be sure."

"I'm fine. Let's get this over with."

I lead the way, but this time, when I walk around the corner, the trailer is gone. The rest of the inspection goes off without a hitch. After going through all the greenhouses, Fleming and Garneau return to the house to go over our records. Meryl pulls up reports on her computer and provides them with copies. She shoots me cold stares, lurking in the background while the inspectors review our data. Moving the plants back and forth makes it appear that our plant count matches the digital records, and they seem satisfied.

As they pack up their things, Fleming summarizes their findings. "Your plant losses are well above the norms. We didn't see anything unusual in the greenhouse environment that would account for so many diseased plants. We suggest you bring in a cannabis production consultant to review your operations and examine your damaged plants. The consultant should be able to advise you on how to reduce your losses."

"Thanks," I say. "That sounds like a good idea. I'll get on that right away."

"You'll get our formal inspection report in a couple of weeks."

From my living room window, I watch them get into their vans and drive off. The tension that has gripped me all day begins to give way. I turn to find Meryl glaring at me.

"You pulled it off this time. How long do you think you can be conning the government before they figure it out?"

"I know. I know. I'll come up with something."

CHAPTER 23

I help Meryl clear the table when everyone finishes eating, leaving the dirty dishes next to the kitchen sink. After returning to the dining room, I decide it's time to kick off the proceedings.

Looking down the table, I realize that all eyes are focused on me, except Ferg, who is eyeballing the plate of desserts. "Can someone pass me the brownies?"

I shake my head. "You've had enough. If they had a breathalyser for sugar, you'd be busted."

"I burn it all off at work."

"How? Riding around in your cruiser?"

"Bite me."

"Dad, is everything alright?" interrupts Sara. "Why all this mystery?"

"Everything is fine. Actually, not really. We have a few issues to deal with. The first being, what to do with all that American cash sitting in my safe. I can't take that much cash to the bank without raising suspicion and triggering anti-money laundering reporting requirements."

"I have a thought," says Sara. "We could each take a portion of the money and take it to different bank branches in the county."

"I don't think so," says Meryl. "How many times can you go back to a branch before people begin to notice?"

I nod in agreement. "I agree. Using the banks isn't going to work."

"Then how about one of those foreign exchange companies?" asks Sara.

"That's not going to work either," I respond, unconsciously tapping a spoon on the table. "They are also covered by anti-money laundering laws. Anyone else have any ideas?"

"I have the solution." We look across at Ferg who is chewing on his fourth brownie. "I recently found out about this guy -"

"Why is it that every idea of yours begins with 'I know a guy'?" asks Meryl, giving him a cold, hard look. "And every time it leads to more problems."

"These aren't problems, just opportunities," says Ferg. "Just minor bumps on the road. Guy will be able to -"

"The guy's name is Guy? Seriously?" I ask.

"Can you shut up and let me finish? Let's say Guy dabbles in foreign exchange. He will be able to convert your money into Canadian funds for a modest commission."

"And are we to believe that Guy is another legitimate entrepreneur like our new partner, Ramone?" asks Meryl, her voice oozing sarcasm.

"What would be his modest commission rate?" I ask.

"I don't know. It could be ten to fifteen percent. Depends on the circumstances."

I grimace and shake my head. "Yeah, very modest. Looks like we don't have many options."

"Why do I have this sick feeling?" asks Meryl. "Could it be that Ferg is hooking us up with another gangster?"

"He's not a gangster and he can help you with this jam."

"That you created, Uncle Ferg," says Sara.

"How does a cop happen to know so many shady characters?" asks Meryl.

"It's an occupational hazard. And why is everyone attacking me? I'm trying to help."

"Stop jumping all over him," I say. "I don't like the idea of getting involved with another illegal deal either. But we need to convert the cash, so, Ferg, you can make the arrangements."

"Consider it done."

"Dad, you said there were other issues," says Sara.

I stand up and pace down the room, gathering my thoughts. "It was a close call with yesterday's inspection. The number of plants disappearing from the inventory for the Michigan buyers is a massive red flag for the regulators. We can't continue to claim these large losses in plants. And then I was thinking, even after we convert all the American cash to Canadian, it's not like we can put it in the bank. It's still a problem."

"So, what's your solution?" asks Sara.

The room is silent, as I continue to pace. I stop and turn to face the group. "The ideal way to continue supplying the Michigan buyers is not to pull product out from our licensed rooms but to set up an unlicensed room."

"Mac!" shouts an exasperated Meryl.

"Hear me out. It's the safest approach. The abandoned barn on the west end of the property that great Grandpa Angus built. It hasn't been used in almost two decades. If we put money into it, we can convert that old eyesore into a functioning grow-op. And the construction money can come out of the cash we have sitting around."

"Sort of sounds feasible," says Sara.

"I like it," adds Ferg.

"Have you people all gone crazy?" howls Meryl, her face reddens and nostrils flare. "Just listen to yourselves. Instead of a plan to get *out* of criminal activity, you're planning to jump in deeper."

"Mom, I don't think we have many options," says Sara. "Don't forget that the future of our farm is at stake."

"You've brainwashed your own daughter," says Meryl. She gets up and storms out of the room. "I want no part of this."

"I'll deal with her later. If we do go forward with this, we'll need to bring in contractors from outside of Norfolk," I add. "We don't want locals to know what we're doing here. They're pissed off enough as it is. We've learned enough about grow-ops that we can direct the contractor on what needs to be built."

"There happens to be a lot of illegal grow-ops still around," notes Ferg. "Maybe we can track down someone who has already built one."

"That barn is so drafty," says Sara. "Wouldn't it make more sense to tear it down and build another greenhouse like the rest of the grow rooms?"

"It would make the most sense. However, people might notice a new greenhouse on the property. Such as government inspectors or Green Fields. No one is going to suspect a grow-op in that rundown barn. We can seal and insulate the inside. It'll mean the plants will grow totally on artificial lighting."

Ferg lets out a snort, nodding his head. "Hiding a grow-op inside a dilapidated barn. The idea is both brilliant and crazy."

"Yeah, it is sort of clever, I must admit," I respond. My pacing only picks up along with my sense of excitement. "This is going to have to be a top-secret operation, especially during the construction phase. So, the fewer people who know, the better. The staff will have to be discrete about what will be happening here."

"How are you going to pull that off?" asks Ferg. "People are going to notice construction vehicles and workers coming and going. You have picketers almost daily now."

"Maybe I'm fixing up this place because I decided to raise a small herd of cows. You know how much I miss dairy farming. As for the picketers, we'll have to coordinate people and material coming in and out with the picketing schedule. They have the damn thing online."

"But think about it, Mac," says Ferg. "Do you really think you can keep all your staff in the dark? You better be prepared to deal with that eventuality."

"I'll deal with it should it come up," I respond.

"Okay. I can help with the contractors," says Sara. "It has to be people who will do this for cash."

"I agree," adds Ferg. "People who accept money under the table are going to keep mum about the work."

From the living room, I hear Mum's voice. "Are you people talking about me?"

I turn my head toward the door where she appears. "No, Mum. What have you been up to?"

"I'm so distressed. Alex has been cheating on Cindi. I knew he was bad news. Her mom wants her to leave him. And to make matters worse, I think she's pregnant again. Haven't those people heard of birth control?"

She traipses into the room and spots the plate of brownies in front of Ferg. "Are those pot brownies?"

CHAPTER 24

I return from town with a load of groceries and enter the property without getting hassled by the protesters. Instead of marching in front of the farm entrance, they are in a scrum circling around Lucille Lamont. It's a bigger group than the usual dozen picketers. There must be at least thirty people milling about.

I stop to check in with Habib, who is inside the property, leaning against the fence. "What's going on over there?"

"I do not know, Mr. McPherson. The people are not marching today. The crazy woman is talking to them for some time. She is up to no good."

"Nothing we can do for now. Keep a close eye on them. Call me if there's any trouble at all."

"Yes, Mr. McPherson."

I drive toward the farmhouse and take the groceries inside. No sooner have I dropped the bags on the kitchen counter when my phone chirps. It's Habib.

"What's up?"

"After you left, the group charged the gate. I could not stop them," the frantic security shouts into the phone. "They are marching to the greenhouses."

"Damn it! Now, they've gone too far. Call the police and I'll head out to intercept them."

I fly up the roadway to the greenhouse and find the mob of devout Lucille followers are outside the mother room banging on the glass walls while chanting "no more weed." Inside, the staff have barricaded themselves to prevent the intruders from entering.

I walk toward them, trying to stay calm. "Everyone, stop!" I shout. I must have startled them because the banging and chanting abruptly ends. "Lucille Lamont, what do you think you're doing?"

She glares at me with her arms crossed. "You know exactly what I'm doing. I'm shutting you down."

I turn to the silly gang. "You should all skedaddle because the police are on the way."

"Don't anyone listen to him," responds Lucille. "No one is going to be arrested."

"We'll see about that," I say as a police cruiser pulls up to the greenhouse in a cloud of dust.

The doors swing open and out step Officers Stutz and Greening. "What seems to be going on here?" asks Nadine.

"As you can see," I begin, "these people have come into my farm and, no doubt, with the intent of destroying property."

"Is that correct, Mrs. Lamont?" asks Bruce, frowning.

"It's no secret what our mission is," she says, stepping forward until she is inches away from the officer's face. "This farm is an abomination, and we will do whatever needs to be done to shut it down."

From around the corner comes Jake with an armful of empty plant pots. "What are you's people doing here?" he asks, dropping the pots at the door to the greenhouse. Then he spots a familiar face. "Hey, Ida. Say hi to your momma."

"I sure will," she responds.

"Jake, this ain't the time for socializing," I growl. "Nadine and Bruce, are you going to do something about this bunch of yahoos?"

Nadine nervously adjusts her ponytail elastics. "Mrs. Lamont, I will have to charge you people with trespassing if he insists on it."

"Do you realize who I am?" asks Lucille, with a quick, disgusted snort. "The Lamonts are pillars in this community."

"Please don't make this difficult," says Nadine, pulling out a notebook. "The law is the law and I'm bound to enforce it. So, either everyone pulls out or I'm going to have to lay charges."

"I'm not going anywhere!" bellows Lucille, crossing her arms.

"Ain't the fine for a conviction as much as $10,000?" I ask.

"Yup," says Bruce. "It's a provincial offense."

Anne Marie grabs Lucille by the arm. "Come on, maybe this isn't such a good idea."

"Harold is going to be really pissed if I get arrested," remarks one woman.

Some of the protesters begin trekking back to the farm entrance. Soon they are all leaving except for Lucille and Anne Marie.

"Mrs. Lamont, why don't you follow these other folks, and we'll call it a day," Nadine suggests.

Lucille puts her arm around Anne Marie, and the two women march defiantly down the road. "This isn't over yet!"

CHAPTER 25

The following evening, I'm lost in thought in front of the television. My demanding "partner" is stressing me out. I've got to find weed to sell him without raising suspicion from the government regulators. Trying to secretly build more capacity is a challenge with the wacky bunch of protesters outside my front gate. Through all this, Meryl is barely speaking to me anymore.

Meryl walks into the room and shuts the television off. "We need to talk."

I let out a sigh. Here comes another boatload of guilt and recrimination. "Sure. What about?"

She stands in front of me with her arms crossed. "I'm worried where this all is heading."

I get up and put my hands on her shoulders. "This is going to work out."

She pushes me away. "Let me see if I have this right. We are falsifying records that we provide to government agencies, illegally selling to American drug dealers, and now you want to get into money laundering. I feel like I'm married to Walter White from *Breaking Bad*."

"You're being overly dramatic."

Meryl picks up a pillow from the couch and throws it at me. "Oh, stop with the farmer 'golly gee' act. We're going to all end up in jail!"

I drop my head and sigh. "Meryl, this is a temporary arrangement. We'll do this for a few months to make up for a slow start up and then go back to a squeaky-clean operation. At some point, the greenhouse that we're going to build in the old west-end barn can be brought online as part of our legitimate business."

"I've still got a bad feeling about this. How many crooks do you think you can do business with before this blows up in your face? I blame Ferg for all this. He's leading us down this road to hell. But you keep going along with everything he suggests, so you're just as bad. If this thing comes unglued, which it probably will, he won't even be able to find work as a supermarket bagger and we will lose everything, including our home."

I sink back into the couch, my shoulders slumping from the crushing weight of her disappointment and anger. "Why don't you calm down and listen to me for a moment?" Meryl remains standing. Her eyes well up. "Everything I've done has only had one objective: to hang onto the family farm. It was never about getting rich."

"No, that's not entirely true. You didn't need to sell any marijuana to Ramone. We would have gotten by."

"Yes, that's true. I never wanted to go into the cannabis business in the first place. But this business isn't as lucrative as it's been made out to be. So, again, I reluctantly agreed to generate additional sales until we are more established and on a better footing. Maybe that was a mistake."

Her eyes roll in response. "Maybe?"

"Yes, it's all illegal and I hate that I'm involved with this. I will end these arrangements within six months. No one is going to be harmed in the interim."

"Okay, you have six months of playing with gangsters," says Meryl in a calm voice, although her fiery stare expresses otherwise. "But after that, if you don't clean this up, I'm walking."

"You do what you have to do. I've got a new grow-op to build and set up."

CHAPTER 26

The smell of coffee and sugary treats hits you the moment you walk into a Tim Hortons. I get into the lunch line, which is at least ten people long and snakes back to the main entrance. The coffee shop is quite busy, and I finally locate Ferg, who already has his food and has snared a table. It takes some time to reach the front of the line to place my order. Fifteen minutes later, I sit down, facing Ferg with my usual Tim Hortons lunch: a soup, chicken sandwich, and coffee. I glance over at Ferg's tray, which is loaded down with fried chicken strips, potato wedges, chili, coffee, and a box of Timbit donuts. "Is that all you're eating? You need to keep up your strength to get through your gruelling schedule."

"What's wrong with this lunch?"

I reach for my sandwich, smirking. "Nothing if your goal is to work part-time as a mall Santa this year."

"The box of Timbits is for a snack later in the day."

"I bet that box doesn't make it out the front door before it's empty."

"Bite me!"

I peak inside my sandwich and make a face. "Ferg, so what's this important news you need to talk to me about?"

Ferg places his plastic fork and knife down on this tray and leans forward so no one around us can hear. "I found out that someone has reported some strange night-time activity at the Port Rowan Marina to the OPP."

"Crap. What does that mean? What's the OPP going to do?"

"Not sure yet. They may only increase patrols in the area. But if they suspect smuggling, they might set up a surveillance team."

"Shit. What am I going to do?"

"Mac, keep your voice down," he whispers, looking around the restaurant to see if anyone is paying attention to us. An old lady at a table next to ours scrutinizes us with a startled look. When she realizes her life isn't in imminent danger, she returns to her own conversation.

"We're dropping off a shipment on Friday."

"Maybe you should cancel it and wait for things to die down. At least until the new year."

Panic sets in and I feel like my lunch is about to come back up. I try to keep my anxiety in check. "Why don't you call Ramone to let him know that we're going to take a break for a couple of months, and see how he reacts to the news?"

"Okay, okay, let me think."

I hold my head in my hands. Various scenarios flash through my mind. In the middle of sales transaction, the police show up to bust me, and I lose my growing license and the farm. Then Ramone is so pissed, he puts a contract out on me. Or how about when the OPP swoop down to make arrests, I get caught in the middle of a shootout between the cops and Ramone's goons. An OPP officer is killed, and I'm charged as an accessory to murder.

"Mac, what do you think?"

"Huh?"

"You haven't been listening to a word I was saying."

I push away the tray with my half-eaten sandwich. "Sorry, I've been busy thinking about how to decorate my prison cell. I should never have listened to you in the first place."

"Chill out, Mac," responds Ferg as he pops another Timbit into his mouth. "Remember, I'm in the OPP. I'll know whether a surveillance team is on duty the night of your next delivery. I'll take care of this from my end."

"Are you sure about this?"

"Trust me."

"Like I have a choice at this point."

Ferg stands up and grabs his OPP bomber jacket hanging from the back of his chair. "I've got to get back to the job."

"Sure thing. Umm, thanks for letting me know."

"You know I got your back."

As Ferg walks toward the door, I look down at the table. "Hey, you forgot your box of donuts."

As he pulls open the door, he turns to look at me. "Nah. The box is empty."

***

On Friday evening, it is unusually warm for November. A fog descends from off the lake as I approach Port Rowan Marina, impairing visibility. The fog is likely a good thing as it will provide us with some cover in case there is anyone around.

Ferg hasn't provided word yet on whether the surveillance team is out tonight. I'm antsy, waiting for his call. My phone rings but I don't recognize the number that pops on the display. I hit the answer button. "Hello."

"Hey, Mac," says Ferg.

"What number is this?"

"I'm using a burner phone."

"What for?"

"Because we aren't having this conversation. Get it?"

"Oh, right. So, what's the story?"

"The surveillance team is out tonight."

"Shit. What do we do?"

"You hang tight until you hear back from me. When I give the all-clear, you can proceed to the pier."

"Okay." After ending the call, I slow the car down and pull off the side of the road.

***

Ferg creeps down Lakeshore Drive until he reaches Dock Street. He's about to turn onto the roadway leading to the marina when he spots the unmarked police vehicle. He pulls up next to the car and gets out of his cruiser. As he approaches the other vehicle, the driver window lowers.

The officer's head leans out the open window. "Ferg, what are you doing out here?"

"Hey Sandy and Randall, I was going to ask you the same thing. I'm doing a patrol of the area and recognized your car parked here."

"We're doing a surveillance of the marina," says Sandy. "There've been reports of suspicious nighttime activity."

"How many nights have you guys been here?"

"This'll be our fifth in the past week," replies Sandy, letting out a yawn.

"Seen anything?"

"It's been dead," says Sandy.

"I think it's someone imagining stuff," adds Randall.

"It could be smugglers or some kids drinking," says Ferg, scratching the side of his head. "You guys looked whacked. I'm happy to finish your shift for you."

Sandy looks over at his partner then back at Ferg. "Gee, I don't know."

"I'm sure you would rather be at home in bed than sitting out here trying to keep each other awake."

"That's for sure," Randall agrees, taking a gulp from a coffee cup. "These stakeouts are painfully boring."

"Then clear out and I'll sit here and stare at the empty pier."

"I don't get it," says Sandy, with raised eyebrows. "Why are you offering to do this? That's not like you, Ferg."

"Look, we're a team. One day you might be able to bail me out of a jam or something like that. Besides, it's only for a few more hours."

Sandy looks over to Randall, who gives Ferg a nod. "Thanks a lot, Ferg. We owe you one."

"No problem. Have a good night, guys."

The other vehicle shifts into gear and drives up Lakeshore Drive. When they're no longer in sight, Ferg pulls out his burner phone.

***

Time seems to move so slowly when you're freaking out. Finally, my phone chirps, and I hit the answer button. "Ferg?"

"Yup. It's all clear now. I see what appears to be a boat light through the fog. It might be your buyers. You don't want to keep them waiting."

"Thanks for this."

"No problem. In the morning, I'll report that I caught some teens drinking and that I gave them a warning before letting them go. That should put an end to the surveillance." The line disconnects before I can respond.

I get back onto Lakeshore Drive and proceed to the marina. When I turn onto Dock Street, I spot Ferg's cruiser parked in a laneway between two buildings. When I reach the dock, I park and turn off the engine. After stepping out of the car, I flip open the trunk and pull out the trash bags filled with cannabis. I stroll down the pier, straining to make out our Michigan contacts through the fog. About three-quarters of the way down the pier, I pick up their voices.

A mammoth of a human being takes a few steps in our direction. "Is that you, McPherson?" He shines the light in my face.

"Yeah." I respond.

"It's so fucking foggy, I can't see for shit," he says. When I get closer, I realize he's got his gun out.

I drop the bags of weed at his feet. "What's with the gun? Were you expecting trouble?"

He picks up the bags and hands me the envelope of cash. "If you had turned out to be someone else, there'd be a big fucking hole in your gut." They climb into the boat, and moments later I'm alone on the pier. That gets me thinking. Maybe I should start bringing a gun down to the pier too.

CHAPTER 27

Two unmarked trucks loaded with construction material slow down as they approach the McPherson farm entrance. The driver of the first truck waits for the line of picketers to move out of the way. When it becomes obvious that they aren't going to move, he leans on his horn. The line in front of the gate refuses to disperse.

He lowers his window and leans his head out. "I gotta get inside. Can you folks move aside?"

Lucille leaves the picket line and struts up to the front of the truck. "We are not going to move. Not until this immoral farm is shut down." She hands the driver a brochure.

"Look, I got no beef with you or anyone else. So, get out of the way."

She shakes her head, turns around, and moves back into the line with the nine other protesters. They march back and forth along the side of the road, singing a church hymn.

The driver of the second truck gets out of his cab and walks over to the first truck. "What the hell is going on?"

"Some protest. They say they ain't moving."

"What are we going to do?"

"I have no idea," says the driver in the lead truck, shrugging his shoulders. "I don't want no trouble."

The gate to the farm swings open, and Habib scampers past the marchers to the trucks. "I am Habib, the security officer. I will get you inside."

The driver looks over at the hymn-singing marchers. "Is it always like this?"

"Most days," Habib answers with a sigh. He leaves the drivers and heads straight to Lucille. "Mrs. Lamont, you know the agreement. You hold up vehicles for no more than five minutes and Habib doesn't call police."

She stops marching and crosses her arms, glaring down at the security officer. "We have no such agreement, little man. You know very well I was coerced into your so-called arrangement by the corrupt police in this county."

"I don't want trouble and you don't either. Move out of the way because I *will* call the police and you'll be fined," he says waving the marchers out of the way.

Lucille sighs as she turns to her group, waving them to one side. "Alright, we have to move. But hold your signs up high with pride."

Habib signals the truck drivers to enter the property. He shuts the gate once they are through, and the picketers resume marching.

***

I finish my coffee and fold up the newspaper I was reading. I look across the kitchen table to Meryl, who is picking at her lunch. "I'm heading over to the old barn to see how the work is coming along."

"Which gangster are you meeting with today?" She doesn't even try to hide her anger. "I can't keep track of them all."

"Ken, the contractor. And, umm…then I meet with Moe, umm…I mean Guy."

She gets up from the table and takes her dirty dishes to the sink. "Wow. Look at you. The big-time money launderer. I think Moe sounds about right. One of the Three Stooges you do business with. Our home sees more criminals than a federal penitentiary."

"I'll see you later, Meryl."

As I drive to the old barn, it still looks like any dilapidated farm structure. The exterior has that country weathered look. The roof has been discreetly replaced to protect the multi-million-dollar operation being set up below. The contractor, Ken (he never gave us his last name), has his truck parked in front of the barn door. His crew is unloading material into the greenhouse.

I wave to the men unloading the truck and walk past them into the nearly completed greenhouse. Inside the barn doors is a second set of insulated and locked doors. We call it a greenhouse, but it's not your classic glassed-in structure. The exterior barn walls have been caulked and sealed. A layer of insulation has been installed to assist the climate control system in maintaining a constant internal temperature. Because we won't be using any natural sunlight, we have had to install a lot of lighting. To reduce our hydro costs, I purchased sets of high-efficient LED lights.

The trickiest part of the construction was running power lines to the greenhouse site. The barn had no electrical service until about a month ago. To avoid suspicion, I had the lines buried underground. Of course, no power company inspector came around to check out the work before the power was hooked up, but everything seems to be working fine. We're on the final stages of construction and should be able to move plants into the greenhouse in a few weeks.

I look across the greenhouse, trying to locate Ken. I finally spot him on a ladder working on the security system. Ken is a small wiry guy in his forties. He's originally from British Columbia and has been working on constructing and setting up grow-ops for about twenty years. When Ken started in the business, none of his clients were legal growers, so he's obviously indifferent to one's legal status. The best part is that Ken asks no questions and will work for cash. And I have plenty of cash.

I stroll over to the ladder where Ken is working. "How's it goin', eh?"

Ken looks down at me. "Hey there." He carefully climbs down the ladder. "Our guys had a hell of a time getting past those crazy people out front."

My head drops as I kick at the debris on the floor. "Sorry about that. I thought they wouldn't be out there. Although their schedule is online, they also make last-minute changes, so we can't be sure exactly what time they will show up."

"If your security guy hadn't intervened, the trucks would have turned around, putting us behind schedule. You need to do something about those people."

I'm thinking that running over a couple of them with a truck might put a scare into them. I have to remember to thank Habib for managing the garbage that goes on out on the road. "There's not much we can do except call the cops if they don't cooperate. How's the work coming along?"

"I've got all the hardware now for the security system, and the Wi-Fi has been set up. I think I'll have the system operating by the end of tomorrow."

I hand him an envelope that he shoves into his pocket. "The last installment will be when all the work is completed."

"That won't take much longer. I still need to put up the walls for your cloning room. It will have a separate lighting and climate control system than the rest of the greenhouse. The control panels are already installed on the wall near that far corner," he says, pointing to the other side of the greenhouse.

"It all looks great, and you've been right on schedule. I appreciate it."

"I've installed the latest technology. You will be able to easily switch the entire room from growing to flowering by adjusting the lighting to the proper spectrum and number of hours."

I nod and pat him on the back. The greenhouse will first be set up for growing, and when the plants are ready to flower, we will adjust the lighting to trigger the flowering process. That means we aren't going to be able to maintain a continuous monthly production of cannabis. We will go months without harvesting. We'll stockpile product so that we can make our monthly shipments to Ramone. If we run short before the next harvest, I'm screwed. The last thing I want is a visit from Ramone.

When I'm done at the construction site, I drive to the greenhouses to examine the flowering rooms. I'm about to remove my overcoat, when one of the employees, Henry, approaches me. "Mr. McPherson, can I talk to you about something?"

Henry has only been with us for two months. He keeps to himself and has been working out okay. "Sure, what's on your mind?"

He avoids looking directly at me, which has me feeling uneasy. "Can we talk outside where we can be more private?"

"Sure." I zip my coat back up and step outside in the cold. I turn and look him straight in the eyes. "What's going on, Henry?"

His face turns dark and his eyes flash. "I know what's going on at the other end of the farm."

I try to remain calm. "What do you think is going on?"

"It's obvious that you're building some grow-op over there. I'm guessing it's not legit."

I have an urge to grab this punk and strangle him right on the spot, but I maintain a blank look. "What does it matter to you?"

An eerie grin appears on Henry's face and his eyes narrow. "I'm guessing that grow-op could be bringing in a lot of loot. Why else would you do it when you got all this? I thought with your extra revenue you might be able to afford more for workers like me."

I shove him with my hand. "You fucking creep! So, you want to blackmail me?"

He grabs my arm and pulls it away from his shoulder. "Look at it as a profit-sharing plan to keep people loyal." My right fist lands on the side of his face and he drops to the icy ground. "And how much would your loyalty cost me?"

He slowly gets up rubbing his cheek. "I'd say about a grand a week should do it." He spits out a mixture of saliva and blood. "But try that again and the price will go up."

I shove my hands in my pocket and head back inside. "I'll get back to you. Now go back to work."

***

It's the end of a long day, and Guy is late for our appointment. When the doorbell chimes, I jump up from the living room couch. The familiar short, scrawny man shuffles inside. With his thinning hair and wire-framed glasses, he looks more like a nerdy accountant than a money launderer (or a money exchanger, as he refers to himself).

Guy is from Birmingham, England and has a heavy Brummie accent, which I sometimes have problems following. He's been living in Canada for close to ten years after what he describes as having a 'row with the ol' lady and got a bit rough with 'er.' She reported him to the police, and he decided it would be a good idea to 'leg it out of the country.' He was a financial analyst in England and continues to work in finance in Canada. Not all his work is legit.

I lead him inside, and he kicks off his shoes. It's well below freezing outside and Guy has on a black peacoat that can't possibly keep him warm. "Can I take your coat?"

"No. I'm fine." That's his usual answer. We shuffle into the kitchen, Guy clinging to his briefcase tucked under his arm.

"Have a seat," I say, pulling out a kitchen chair. "Can I get you something to drink? Coffee, soft drink, water?"

"No, ta. I ay stayin' lung." Also, his standard response.

Once seated, he puts his briefcase on the table. He removes his glasses - which have fogged up when he came inside from the frigid dry air - and wipes the lenses with a corner of his shirt.

Meryl stands silently by the sink, glaring at Guy. He shoots her a weak smile that she refuses to acknowledge. He clears his throat and returns his attention to me. "Yow said yow 'ad fifty thousan' U.S. dollurs."

"That's right," I say, pulling out a stack of American dollars from a canvas bag on the seat next to me and placing it on the table.

Guy picks up his phone and opens his calculator app. "The exchaynge rayte taday is wun dollur an' thirty-thray cents. That werks owt ter sixty-six thousan', thray undred an' eighty Canadian doll-urs. Less me commission, yow net fifty-eight thousan', thray hundred an' twenty-foive dollurs."

"Sure thing."

He flips open his briefcase and pulls out a several bundles of hundred-dollar bills. "Thems bundles o' ten thousan'," he says pushing five stacks of bills. He pulls apart another bundle and counts until he reaches eighty-three. He then pulls out twenty-five dollars from a roll of cash in his pocket. "There yer goo. Yow can count it mek shoo-er."

I toss the stacks of bills into my bag.

Guy watches with a confused look on his face. "Ay yow goo-in ter count the munnay?'

I get up from the table. "It's fine. Umm, thanks for coming by, and I'll be in touch when I have more to exchange."

He grabs his briefcase and follows me to the front door. "Sure."

I hold the door open for him while he bends down to put on his shoes. As soon as he steps outside, I fling the door shut. As I spin around to return to the kitchen for the cash, I find Meryl standing in the entrance way with her arms across her chest, blocking my path.

"What now?" I ask.

"I can't believe you invite these criminal and low-lifes into our home."

"I don't have time for this," I say, squeezing my way past her to the kitchen. I grab the bag of cash on the kitchen table and scurry to the office where we keep our safe.

Meryl follows me down the hallway. "I don't know you anymore."

"Don't be so melodramatic," I say, spinning the dial on the safe. "You know we're only doing this until we can get more financially secure."

"Secure?" she says, her voice screeching. "I've never felt less secure in my life."

I bend down to stack the bills in the safe.

CHAPTER 28

After sleeping on it, I decide that paying off Henry is my only option. I'm going to have to keep an eye on him from now on. I hope no one else decides to get involved in this extortion game. But, for now, I have more than enough to deal with.

I expect Jimmy to drop by this morning for an update. I had wanted to do this over the phone, but he insists on coming over. Right now, the last thing I need is more anxiety. I grab a bottle of antacid tablets sitting on the bathroom vanity and swallow two. My gut has been in turmoil for weeks.

I step out onto the porch when I hear the crunch of tires on the snow-covered gravel on our driveway. The cold breeze sends a shiver through my body.

"Hey, Jimmy, how's it goin', eh?"

"I'm good, Mac."

"Why don't you come in from the cold?"

"Grab your coat, and we can head over to the greenhouses. I wanted to check in and see how things are going."

"I'll be right with you." I pull my coat out of the front closet and put on my boots. Once outside, I dig out my keys. "Hop in my truck and we can drive over together."

"Sounds good," responds Jimmy. He yanks open the passenger door and gets in. "I noticed some construction activity on the far side of the farm. What's going on over there?"

Oh, crap. He noticed. "It's a...not a big deal. Umm, we have a barn down there that's in bad shape. And umm, it's the original barn built by my great grandfather."

"In the middle of winter? That's an unusual time to be doing this type of work."

"It's literally falling apart. A strong wind could bring it down, so we decided it couldn't wait," I say, trying to think of something to change the subject. "That's quite a storm we had last week."

"It wasn't so bad. Can we ride over to see the barn?"

"I, umm...would love to take you over. But the contractor is so temperamental. He doesn't like people visiting his construction sites."

"That's ridiculous," says Jimmy frowning. "It's your property."

"Yeah, I know," I say with sigh. "But he does good work, is quite reasonable, and is hard to book. It's one of those times where you just accept it."

"It's still bullshit. I'm sure we could have found you a contractor as good as your guy."

"Next time I'll take you up on the offer." We arrive at the greenhouses, and I park the truck. "What would you like to see?"

Stepping out of the vehicle, he turns to the first greenhouse, which happens to be a vegetation room. "This is good enough place to start."

Once inside the greenhouse, we stomp the snow off our boots and slip booties over them. We are about to do a walkaround when I spot Mum wandering down one of the aisles.

"Mum, what are you doing here?" I call out. She turns and waves at us then continues down the aisle.

We follow and catch up to her at the far end of the greenhouse. "Mum, what are you up to?"

"Son, I decided to visit the greenhouse to pick some flowers for the house. It needs some color. But none of these plants are flowering yet," she says, shaking her head. "What a disappointment."

"That's because these aren't flowering plants. Meryl can take you into town to buy some flowers."

"What's the point of growing plants with no flowers?" She stomps back down the aisle towards the entrance.

"Is she serious?" asks Jimmy, raising his eyebrows. "She doesn't know these are marijuana plants?"

I sigh. "Mum does confuse things every so often."

"Managing her must be tough on the family."

"I admit she exhausts us at times," I say, dropping my voice. "So, anything that you want to see?"

"Nothing in particular." Jimmy strolls around the room, looking at plants while I follow. "In fact, everything looks great."

"We've made it through our growing pains. Excuse the pun," I say, grinning. "But there must be a reason why you dropped by today."

"I did want to raise one issue with you," he says. His demeanor changes from friendly to something more serious. "We recently received copies of reports from the feds indicating an unusual plant loss rate."

"Yeah. We couldn't trace the problem, but they didn't find much and made a few suggestions."

"This is your farm, and we don't want to interfere, but we have more than a passing interest in what goes on here," he says, taking some photos with his phone. "I want to remind you that we are always available to provide some advice. I can send someone over to help out."

"I think we're fine now, but I'll definitely keep that in mind."

"Mr. McPherson."

I turn around to find Jake standing there, his eyes locked on Jimmy.

"Yeah, what's up?" I ask.

He continues to stare, shifting from side to side. "Umm, sir, it's kind of personal."

"As you can see, I'm with Jimmy," I say, grimacing. "Can it wait?"

"Hello, Jake," says Jimmy.

"Hey there, Mr. Scarpini. Umm, sorry, Mr. McPherson, but it can't wait."

"Excuse me, Jimmy."

We walk over to the entrance. Jake is still observing Jimmy as he leans closer to my ear to whisper. "There's a problem at the old barn. That guy Ken told me to get you."

"Gotcha. I'll get over there as soon as I get rid of Jimmy."

"Do you need me to do anything?"

"Yes. Stop staring at Jimmy. You're creeping him out."

"Sorry, Mr. McPherson."

Jake leaves and I return to Jimmy. "Is everything alright?"

"Everything is fine. Jake wanted to ask for some time off. But, with him, everything is so dramatic."

About twenty minutes later, I finish with Jimmy and drive him back to his car. As he drives away, I rush back to my vehicle and slip on some ice, falling on my face. When I lift myself off the ground, blood is dripping down my face from a gash on my forehead. I hope this doesn't turn out to be another fucked-up day. Holding a tissue to my forehead, I rush over to the old barn. *Please no more surprises.*

When I walk in, there is no activity, and the barn is in total darkness. Ken is standing around with his workers drinking coffee.

"It's about time you got here," he says, frowning. "Shit. What happened to you?"

"Sorry, but I was tied up with someone and then I fell on my face. Why is it dark in here?"

"We lost all power."

"Can you fix it?"

"I'm not sure. It may have to do with the hookup to the outside line."

I unconsciously rub my forehead, which starts the blood to flow again. "That doesn't sound good. We can't call up the power company to check their end."

"No shit. I'm trying to get hold of a guy who used to work for the power company. I'm hoping he can figure out what's wrong. Other than that, I don't know what else to do."

"I supposed you have no idea when the power will be restored."

Ken shakes his head. "It would be nice if we can get it going by the end of the day. But that depends on when I hear back from my guy and when he can get over here. Not much we can do around here until we get back power."

"Are you sure this guy can be trusted and knows what he's doing?"

"You got any other ideas?"

I grab a piece of lumber and toss it across the barn. "That's what I pay you for. Just get it fixed."

"Relax. My guy will get you power."

CHAPTER 29

Driving past the Dominion bank branch in Delhi, I peer through the front windows. Desmond sits in his office, chatting with a customer…or maybe it's his next victim. His ridiculous comb-over is visible even from a moving vehicle. I'm still fuming over the treatment I received from him and the bank. It's been almost two years since I sat in his office where he literally pulled the rug from under us and put an end to our dairy farm. Thank God my dad is no longer around.

If only we were still in the dairy business. Now that is an honest profession. Like I've always said, agriculture is the backbone of this country.

I turn the corner at the next intersection and drive another block before pulling into the Walmart parking lot. The morning sun is melting the huge mounds of black snow left after a winter of plowing, revealing the dirt and garbage mixed in with the snow. Filthy puddles formed in depressions in the asphalt surface. I find a dry, vacant parking space and back my truck into it.

As I walk toward the store entrance, I reach into my pocket, pull out Meryl's shopping list, and grab an empty shopping cart. Inside, I work my way up the aisles and down Meryl's list. Somewhere between kitchenware and electronics, I hear a voice from behind. "Preston McPherson, Delhi's sinning farmer. We don't see you and Meryl in church anymore."

I spin around to find a smirking Anne Marie. "Well, if it isn't one of Lucille Lamont's disciples. Yeah, the church hasn't exactly been a supportive environment."

I try to push my cart by her. "You will find support through salvation," she retorts, her nose up in the air.

"I'll keep that in mind. So, are you picking up more poster board and markers for next week's protest?"

"Don't worry, we have plenty supplies for signs."

I shake my head in frustration and continue pushing my cart. "Why don't you women give up? No one beyond your little cult gives a rat's ass about what I'm growing."

"Because the Lord cares. But He will forgive your sinning even though you're doing the devil's work!" she calls out. I don't bother to acknowledge her. I'm tired of being harassed by this moralistic band of Bible thumpers. I hate coming into town. I grab the last few items on the list and make a beeline for the checkout. When it's time to pay, I pull out my wallet and look down at the wad of one hundred-dollar bills. I pull two out and hand it to the cashier.

At home, I drop the shopping bags on the kitchen table, grabbing one and pulling out a bag of rice to put away. Meryl picks up one of the other bags. I feel an awkward quiet in the room. After several minutes of the silent treatment, I decide to say something. "What's on your mind?"

"Who says I've got something on my mind?"

"I did. Let's not play games. Come out and tell me."

She puts down a box of dishwasher detergent. "Six months ago, we had a discussion about where the business was going."

"We've had many discussions about the farm."

"Yes, we have, but on this occasion, I spoke to you about the criminal activity we've become involved in. Selling drugs to American dealers. Smuggling. Money laundering. Setting up an illegal growing operation."

"Okay."

Her dark brown eyes fill with sadness as she speaks. I know where this is going. "You promised you would put an end to the illegal stuff in six months. It's now beyond six months and nothing has changed."

I slide down into a kitchen chair and stare at the floor to avoid her dejected look. I struggle to find the right words. "It's not a good time. Let's be honest, your six-month timeline was always unrealistic."

Meryl slams the box of detergent on the counter. "Then you should have said so back in October!"

"This is our life right now. No one is forcing you to stay."

***

The black Cadillac Escalade creeps down the road in front of the McPherson farm. Between the car and the entrance is a band of nine women doggedly waving protest signs.

Ramone, who is sitting in the back, leans forward in his seat. "What the fuck is this?"

"No clue, boss," says Angel as he leans on the horn.

Instead of moving aside, Lucille directs the women toward the front of vehicle and has them lock their arms to form a human barrier.

The driver lowers his window and leans his head out the window. "We gotta go inside. Get outta the way."

The women tighten their grip on each other and hold their ground. Lucille calls out to the driver. "No one is getting through. As far as we know, you could be one of those drug-peddling heathens."

The driver looks back at Ramone. "What should we do?"

"Get them bitches out of the way!"

The SUV pulls over to the side of the road, and the driver steps out. Habib has been watching the scene from his car on the other side of the gate. When he realizes a confrontation is about to occur, he darts out of his car to intervene. He scoots past the ladies to intercept the driver. "Please do not start trouble. I will get you inside."

He peers down at Habib. "Who the fuck are you?"

"I am Habib. Mr. McPherson's security officer."

A smirk spreads across his face. "I won't be needing no help in moving them."

"Please, I do not want any trouble," says Habib, trying to direct the driver back to the SUV.

Ramone pokes his head out a window. "Angel, shove them the fuck out of the way."

"No, no, no," Habib pleads as the driver pushes him out of the way.

The thug marches to the group of women huddled together in front of the gate to the farm. "Now, I'm gonna tell you one more time only. Get outta the way or y'all gonna find yourselves lying in that ditch over there."

"We're not afraid of you!" shouts Anne Marie, holding her phone in one hand. "Get back in your car or I'm calling the police."

He breaks out laughing. "Yeah, go right ahead and call the cops."

Lucille steps forward and puts her arm around Anne Marie. "Don't worry, I've already put in a call. I'm sure they'll be interested in knowing why hoodlums with Michigan plates are visiting this sinful place."

"Please, lovely ladies, you have to move from in front of the gate?" pleads Habib. "I want no trouble. Please no trouble."

Frustrated by all this nonsense, Ramone steps out of his vehicle and stomps over to the scrum. At six feet and three inches, he's an intimidating man dressed in a black Dolce & Gabbana suit with a matching black shirt, Stemar boots and a pair of Ray-Ban sunglasses. He has no coat on despite the cool April weather.

He stops directly in front of Lucille. "I got business to attend to here, and you ladies are holding me up." Habib tries to step in between Ramone and Lucille, but the drug dealer pushes him away.

The group goes silent until Lucille speaks up. "Really, and what type of business are you in?"

Ramone grabs the placard in her hands and repeatedly smashes it against the asphalt surface until the wood stake splinters. Lucille flinches with each swing but holds her ground.

In the distance, the wail of a police siren can be heard. "The police are coming, Mister Tough Guy, so for your own good, I'd leave now," says a defiant Lucille.

The siren grows louder, and eventually two police cruisers with flashing lights arrive and pulls over onto the shoulder of the road. Out steps Ferg from the first police car. Officers Stutz and Greening step out of the other cruiser.

Nadine scrambles over to speak to Ferg with Bruce following right behind. "What's going on here?"

"Guys, it's these damn protesters again from the church. They're harassing everyone trying to get inside the farm."

She straightens out her cap, tucking some loose strands of hair under the brim. "You need any help?"

"Yeah. Stick around. For a while, this bunch was beginning to lose interest in their protest, but recently they've become bolder and more confrontational." He hikes up his trousers and marches toward the combatants. "Okay, what seems to be the problem?"

Everyone begins to talk at once, trying to explain their version of the events. Ferg looks down at the ground, shaking his head. "Everyone shut up!" He points to Habib. "What's your story?"

"These gentlemen are trying to enter farm, but ladies not letting them through."

"Gentlemen? They're obviously gangsters. Look at them," says Anne Marie, puffing out her chest.

"Did I ask you to speak? No, I didn't, so zip it," barks Ferg. He points to Lucille. "Did you block this vehicle from entering the farm?"

"Yes!" she declares. "Sergeant Becker, must I remind you that you are paid to support the community, not hoodlums?"

"I'm paid to enforce the law. That includes, public disturbance, unlawful assembly and highway traffic violations."

"What an outrage! This man destroyed my sign without any provocation," shouts Lucille, pointing at Ramone.

Ferg turns to Ramone. "What do you have to say about this?"

"Sergeant, we're here visiting Mr. McPherson's farm to learn about his operations. My associate and I are from Michigan and eager to learn about cannabis farming. As for the sign, I was concerned that these agitated women would poke someone's eye out."

Ferg shifts his weight back and forth from one leg to the other. He has no clue why Ramone is here but can't come out and ask him in front of everyone. "I need to see your driver's license and vehicle ownership registration."

Ramone nods his head toward Angel who trots back to their vehicle. "My associate will get that for you." When he returns, the driver hands the documents over to Ferg.

Ferg examines the two pieces of identification and then hands them back. "Okay, everything looks in order. I want you all to clear out of the way and let this vehicle in. You know that you aren't supposed to hold vehicles for more than five minutes."

"What?" declares Lucille, her eyeballs bulging. "Aren't you going to check for arrest warrants or something like that?"

"The only arrest that I'm going make will be you, if you don't move," says Ferg.

She thrusts her wrist forward. "Then go right ahead, Becker, and arrest me."

"If that's the way you want to play. Fine." Ferg pulls out his handcuffs and slaps them on her wrists. He waves over at Bruce. "Take her downtown and have her husband come and pick her up."

"Are you sure you want to be doing this?" asks Bruce as he grabs Lucille's arm.

"She's been warned enough times," says Ferg as Bruce takes her to their cruiser. Nadine pushes Lucille's head down, so it doesn't bang on the door frame while putting her in the backseat.

"This is an outrage!" screams Lucille as Nadine slams the door shut. "Look at those two. They're the criminals."

As the cruiser pulls away, Ferg turns toward the mob. "Anyone else want to spend some time in a jail cell?" No one steps forward. "I didn't think so."

He turns to Ramone before getting into his cruiser. "I don't think you'll have a problem now."

Ramone approaches Ferg. "So, we can go in now?"

"Follow me. I'll even escort you in."

"Thank you, Sergeant," replies Ramone as a smile spreads across his face, revealing his gold grill.

CHAPTER 30

As I put away a recent order of office supplies, the door chimes ring. We aren't expecting anyone. My gut tightens up, and I search the counter for my antacid tablets. When I swing the door open, I find Ramone, Angel, and Ferg standing in front of me. I feel like throwing up. "Is something wrong? Why are you all here?"

"These two were experiencing some difficulty getting past your fan club out front," says Ferg. "I finally cuffed Lucille and had her charged."

"Desmond is going to be pissed at you."

"Are they always here?" asks Ramone, looking around the house.

"Most days."

"So, ain't you going to invite us in?" asks Ramone.

I step aside and they stroll into the living room where Mum is watching one of her soap operas. She looks up and gawks at the two visitors. "Why are the undertakers here?" she asks with wide eyes.

"What are you talking about?" responds Ramone.

"You heard me, Blake! I'm not ready to meet my maker yet."

I shake my head at the confused men. "Sorry. She's referring to characters in her TV shows."

Meryl calls from the kitchen, "Who was at the door?" She walks through the living room on the way to the office and stops dead in her tracks when she spots the visitors.

"Good afternoon," says Ramone, bowing his head slightly. "You must be the lovely wife."

"Umm, this is...Ramone and...Angel," I splutter, forcing a smile. "And this is Meryl."

"Okay," she says, crossing her arms, frowning. "Why are you here?"

"Yes…umm, why *are* you here?" I repeat. "I'm sort of surprised to see you."

"Yeah, what gives?" says Ferg.

Ramone looks over at his colleague and smiles. "You people are so suspicious. We've been doing business for all these months, and I realized Angel and me have never seen your farm. As you have so eloquently stated before, agriculture is the backbone of your country. Ain't that right?"

"Yeah, I guess I say that a lot. Sure, I can show you around the farm."

"Marvelous."

"Ferg, are you going to join us?"

"No, I'm going back to work. I'm going to have to deal with Lucille. Besides, I've seen your operation before."

"Ferg, you don't need to run back to work right away," I say, discreetly grinding my heel into his toes. "Do you?"

"Oww, umm…no. I'm not in any hurry."

"Good," I reply. "Let's all head out. Shall we?" I grab a jacket and my shoes and lead the way.

As we walk across the parking lot, I catch a glimpse of Bess who has been lurking at the side of the house. Like a good guard dog, she suddenly bolts for Ramone and Angel and blocks their path.

"What the hell?" bellows Angel. He steps backward and draws his gun, which shakes in his hand.

"*Mooooo.*"

"Angel, put your gun away," orders Ramone.

Meryl moves to Bess and puts her arms around her neck. "Hey, baby, no one is going to hurt you."

"I'm sorry, Mrs. Mac, but your animal has alarmed my colleague," says Ramone grinning. "I assume he's not dangerous."

"He is a *she*, and no, she's not," says Meryl, stroking Bess' backside. "Mommy and Daddy will be back soon. You just relax by the house."

"*Mooooo.*"

I unlock our Ford Explorer, and everyone piles in. Meryl sits in the front with me while Ferg is sandwiched between Ramone and Angel. I point to the cluster of greenhouses. "Straight ahead is where all the growing takes place."

I escort the two visitors through the greenhouses as I've done for so many others over the past eighteen months. Tour guide should be included in my job description. About forty-five minutes into the walk about, I wrap up, eager to see them leave. "As you can see, because we are licensed, we are limited on how much we can sell to you without raising suspicion."

"This is very impressive Mr. Mac," notes Ramone as we trudge back to my car. Then he points to the west end of the farm. "What's that over there?"

"It's just an old barn," I say, pulling open the car door.

"That barn has the unlicensed stuff," says Ferg.

I was tempted to grab his service revolver and put a bullet through his near empty head for that remark.

"There's more?" asks Ramone.

"Mac isn't selling you weed from the licensed rooms. He has a separate room for that."

"Interesting. We would like to see that."

I punch Ferg in the arm when the others are looking. "Umm, it's on the other side of the farm and it doesn't look any different than these rooms. It's a small operation."

"You are too modest, Mr. Mac," says Ramone with a creepy grin spread across his face. "Angel, aren't you curious to see the other grow room?"

"I sure am, boss."

"Well, that settles it," says Ramone, pointing to the door. "Lead the way, Mr. Mac."

When the two thugs step outside, I pull Ferg aside. "What the fuck is wrong with you?"

"What's wrong with *you?* What are you so uptight about?"

"Because the less these criminals know about my business, the better. I had you stick around for support, not to hang me out to dry."

Ferg rolls his eyes as he heads to the door. "You worry too much."

Once everyone returns to the car, I follow the road that goes to the barn at the west end of the farm. I look over at Meryl who has been quiet. Too quiet. I pull up to the front of the barn. "Here we are."

"This is just a run-down barn," says Ramone, shrugging his shoulders.

"That's what it used to be," I say. "Inside is a fully functioning grow-op."

Stepping out of the car, Ramone nudges Angel with his elbow. "These are clever people we are partnered with."

That produces a scowl from Meryl. The last thing she needs to hear is that her business associates are criminals. After entering through the front door, Ramone scans the building with his mouth agape. "You are far too modest, Mr. Mac. This is brilliant!"

"It's not so brilliant, but it works," I say.

"Angel, look at this. State of the art lighting and a high-end climate control system."

"Looks amazing, boss."

"Your yields must be off the charts."

"They're pretty good."

"I want to double our monthly purchases."

Meryl who has been quiet up to now steps forward shaking her head. "That's not possible. Besides this is a temporary set up."

"But it *is* possible, Mrs. Mac, and it's going to happen. We're partners, remember?"

"We're not partners," she responds, grimacing.

Ramone lets out a deep sigh. "Of course, we are. And we will ensure that nothing bad will happen to your farm as long as our partnership remains intact. Ain't that right, Angel?"

Angel puffs out his chest and nods.

"Are you making a threat?" asks Ferg, pointing a finger at Ramone. "You're in Canada. This isn't your home turf."

Ramone grins and shakes his head. "Sergeant, what are you going to do about it? Are you going to report to your superior that you've been supporting an illegal drug operation? And Mr. Mac, those charming ladies marching in front of your farm would love to know about what really goes on here. No. I think not."

None of us say anything. I feel like I'm going to throw up.

"I think we've seen enough here, and we need to get back to Michigan," says Ramone. "We would appreciate a ride back to our car."

We shuffle back to my SUV and return to the house in silence. I park next to their Escalade. Before exiting, Ramone says, "Thank you for the enlightening tour and your hospitality. I expect to see the increased shipments begin this month." They slip out of my car and moments later drive off.

When their car disappears, Meryl explodes. "You fucking idiots! You've put our family in danger!" Tears stream down her red face.

"Let's not get hysterical," responds Ferg. "We'll find a way out of this."

"Does a way out involve more criminals? Because apparently they are the only people you know these days!"

"I know I fucked up, but I'm going to help you get out of this jam," says Ferg.

"Fuck you! You've done enough," she sputters out between sobs. "I'm done. I'm packing my things and moving out."

CHAPTER 31

I open one eye to check the time. Shit. I've overslept. Rolling over onto my back, I rub my face. As I become aware of my surroundings, I realize there's a persistent banging in the background. It's someone pounding on my front door.

I lower my feet to the floor and feel around for my slippers. I slide my feet in and grab my housecoat before plodding to answer the nonstop banging. "Umm, Desmond, what are you doing here?"

He barges past me. "You, vindictive prick. How dare you have my wife arrested?"

I'm still groggy from sleep and have no desire to get into this. "Good morning to you, too."

"Poor Lucille was handcuffed and dragged away in front of members of our church. She is totally humiliated."

"Listen, you pencil-necked geek, I never called the police. *She* did. She's been picketing in front of my home and business, harassing visitors, employees, and friends for nine months. I haven't done squat to stop her. Ain't my fault she crossed the line and got arrested."

He waves a finger in my face. I have to hold back from grabbing it and snapping it in two. "You don't fool me, Preston. I know you worked this out with your corrupt brother-in-law. You will all pay for this."

By now I'm no longer drowsy. My skin is flushed and my body shakes. I step forward and give him a shove. He doesn't expect it and topples over. "No one comes into my house and threatens me. Get out before I knock the crap out of you."

He scrambles to his feet and dashes to the door. "You've not heard the last from the Lamonts," he bellows as he runs to his car for safety. I slam the door shut.

***

I've taken over the bookkeeping functions since Meryl walked out. Sara says her mom lives with her sister in Toronto until she finds a place of her own. I've had no communication with her and not interested in having any. She's abandoned us.

Managing the farm remains a challenge. The farm has begun to finally turn a decent profit, but now I'm having problems balancing the demands of our legal and black-market clients. I now meet weekly with Sara to go over the numbers. Ferg occasionally drops by to provide moral support.

Both are present this evening as we go over the latest spreadsheets. They stare at the paper spread across the dining room table in front of them. The only sounds in the room are Ferg taking sips from his coffee mug and the pen clicking in my hand. I stare at the tip retracting in and out.

Sara clears her throat. "Dad, this doesn't look right. It shows you're short of product this month."

"Yeah. I thought the barn grow-op would eliminate this problem," adds Ferg.

"You're both right," I say. "We are going to be short of product this month and it wasn't supposed to happen again. Now that Ramone has increased his monthly purchases, not enough barn weed has flowered to meet the demand. So, we're back to a shortage situation until we catch up a month or two."

"Can't you tell them to wait until we have enough?" asks Sara.

My head drops and a let out a sigh. "I wish it were that simple. But these people negotiate with a gun pointed at your head."

"What about telling Green Fields you're short or delaying their shipment?" asks Sara.

"That's going to raise too much suspicion," I reply, still clicking my pen. "They've already expressed concern about our inventory issues. They'll want to know how we could possibly be short. The last thing I want is for them to come around to review our inventory. And we have the inspectors to worry about, too. At any time, they can pop up out of the blue."

Sara slaps her open hand on the table. "I know! Remember the break-in last year?"

"What about it?" I ask.

"Why don't we fake another break-in?"

I put down the pen and stroke my chin. "That might be tough to pull off."

"I agree. Can't work," says Ferg as he pushes his coffee mug away. "You've got upgraded security, video cameras everywhere, and security staff. Too messy."

"Does the staged robbery have to take place on the farm?" asks Sara.

"I think you're on to something," I say, jumping out of my seat. "We could stage a robbery."

"Where are you going with this?" asks Ferg.

I pace up and down the room. "A staged break-in would be too difficult to pull off."

"But the weed is all here," says Ferg. "It never leaves the farm until it's shipped to…I get it -"

"We stage a hold-up delivering weed to Green Fields on the twenty-second. That will give us enough weed to delivery to our other buyer on the twenty-sixth."

"This is crazy enough to work," says Ferg. "But if you think you're going to include me in this, forget it. I can't be involved in reporting the robbery or investigating it."

"It doesn't have to be Uncle Ferg, right?" asks Sara.

"I agree that it's better if you're not involved," I say as my pacing picks up speed. "We're going to treat it as an actual crime and report it through the usual channels."

"I'll make sure that Nadine and Bruce are on duty that day," says Ferg, nodding his head. "They gotta be the most gullible cops in the detachment."

"Are we sure this is going to work?" asks Sara. "It's going to have to be planned down to the last detail and be cleanly executed. It's not going to be easy to fool the police."

"Who's going to be the driver?" asks Ferg.

"Jake has usually been driving the shipments over to Green Fields," adds Sara.

"No, it's not going to be Jake," I say. "Not that he can't be trusted, but can you see him trying to keep the story straight?"

"You're right," Sara agrees. "He'd mess it up for sure."

I drop my gaze down to Ferg. "It will have to be me. Ferg, how do we make sure your cops don't ask too many questions?"

"You don't have to worry about these two."

"Let's start working on the details."

CHAPTER 32

Jake throws the sealed bags of marijuana into the back of the panel truck and climbs into the driver's seat. The truck heads down Regional Road 4 toward Green Field in Brantford. The road is virtually empty. Several minutes before reaching the county line, Jake pulls off the road and onto the shoulder, parking behind me.

I hop out of my car and hand Jake a pair of gloves. "Are you ready?"

"Sure thing, Mr. McPherson."

We walk to the back of the truck, and I pull open the doors. "Why do I need to be wearing gloves?" asks Jake, staring down at his gloved hands.

I grab the bags of marijuana and trudge back to my vehicle. "I don't want your fingerprints on the back door of the truck. I expect the police will try to get a set of prints."

"Gotcha. But I use the truck. Wouldn't they expect to find my prints on it?"

I toss the bags into my vehicle and pull out a roll of duct tape. "Let's play this like it really happened."

"Sure thing," says Jake, looking around. "I'm kind of new at this. What do I do?"

"When I put my hands behind my back, you tie them together with tape. And hurry up before someone passes by." Jake follows my instructions and, with my palms together, wraps several layers of duct tape around my wrists until they are snug. Then he bends down and does the same to my ankles.

"Can you get in alright?" he asks.

"Yup." I hop to the open backdoor of the truck and sit down on the floor. Jake grabs my legs and swings them inside.

"I'll see you later, Mr. McPherson." He slams the door shut and trots back to my car. I can hear Jake starting the other vehicle and driving it off the gravel shoulder onto the roadway.

Unable to check my watch, I resort to counting as a way of estimating how much time has passed. The plan is for me to work myself free and call the police. I squirm about on the floor trying to find a comfortable position. After enough time has passed for Jake to get back to the farm, I try to wiggle my wrists free. It doesn't turn out to be that simple. With my arms behind his back, I can't create enough force to free myself. Maybe we should have done a practice run. After several minutes of struggling, my shoulders go numb. Trying to pull my legs free also ends in frustration.

I slump onto the truck floor covered in sweat. "Grrr! Did you have to do such a fucking good job?" I scream. Exasperated, I raise my bound feet and kick at the side panels. "HELP!" The noise echoes through the truck interior. I hear the occasional vehicle roar past. After several minutes of banging and yelling, I give up on this as well. "I'm going to fucking kill Jake if I ever get out of this truck."

I struggle to flip over into a sitting position, so that my knees are bent, and the soles of my feet are on the floor. From that position, I slide my body several inches forward before toppling over onto my side. Once again, I manage to get back onto my butt and repeat the manoeuvre. After several attempts, my feet are within reach of the back door. Next, I lay on my back and raise my feet onto the door latch. My feet push down the latch until the lock disengages. At the same time, I thrust my legs into the door causing it to spring open.

The rest should be easy from here. I roll toward the open door and fall out of the truck, landing face first onto the gravel below. "Ouch!" I roll over onto my side, spitting out gravel from my mouth. I struggle to get to my feet but only get as far as a kneeling position. Realizing that getting to my feet is impossible, I lay down onto my side again, roll to the edge of the road, and return to my knees.

I picked this stretch of road because it's not busy. That was a plus when we were setting up the robbery scene. The situation quickly becomes frustrating after several minutes pass without a single vehicle driving by. Pain shoots through my legs caused by sharp pieces of gravel digging into my knees. A car approaches on the other side of the road. I straighten up and raise my head high to make myself as visible as possible and shout, "Help…help!" The car zooms past me. I feel a drop on my head. And then several more. "Fuck, it's raining!"

Soon I'm soaked and shivering. Cars whiz by and either the drivers don't see me or want nothing to do with me. No one stops. The pain in my shoulders becomes worse and now my legs cramp. Why did I think this was a good idea? I should have let Jake be the hijack victim.

I'm close to tears and chilled from the cold rain when I spot a van heading toward me. The driver slows down as he catches sight of me and pulls up behind the truck. He leaps out of his vehicle and runs over to me. "Hey, are you alright?"

"Thank God you stopped. I'm fine. Can you get me free?"

"Of course," he replies, bending down to pull strips of tape from my wrists. "What happened?"

"Damn it, I was robbed." Enough tape has been removed to allow me to wiggle my wrists loose. "I can get my legs free. Can you call the police?"

"For sure," he says, grabbing his phone from his back pocket.

While the driver is on the phone with the police dispatcher, I work at getting my legs free. I grumble to myself that Jake must have used a half a roll of tape. Jesus Murphy, maybe he was worried I would get free too quickly.

After calling 9-1-1, he puts away his phone. "The police should be here soon."

"Thanks again for stopping. I'm Preston."

"I'm Craig. So, would you like me to stick around until the police arrive?"

"Yeah, that would be great," I say. "Oh, shoot. I better call my family. I need to tell them what's happened and that I'm okay." I remove my phone from my back pocket and dial.

"I've got some bad news, Sara. I was robbed and they stole the entire shipment."

"Have the police shown up yet?"

"I'm fine. The police have been called but they're not here yet."

"Great. Any problems getting free?"

"I'm a little shaken up. They tied me up and had a hell of a time getting free."

"Umm, it sounds like you're not alone."

"I was fortunate that a Good Samaritan stopped to help me. I'll call you after the police show up."

"Talk to you later."

"Sure thing."

In the distance, I make out the flashing lights of a police cruiser tearing down the highway toward us. I put away my phone as the cruiser pulls up behind Craig's van. I look over at him and say, "Umm, will you be able to stick around to give the police a statement?"

"Yeah, no problem. I'm in no hurry."

Two Norfolk police officers step out of the cruiser and march toward us. As promised by Ferg, it's Nadine and Bruce. This seems to be working out fine.

"Preston, what seems to be the problem?" asks Nadine.

"What the hell. I was held up and had a shipment of cannabis stolen."

"Jesus Murphy." Then Nadine glances over to Craig. "And who are you?"

"Craig Summers. I happened to be driving by and seen him on the ground tied up with duct tape."

Nadine scratches the side of her head and straightens her cap. "Bruce, why don't you get a statement from this nice feller, and I'll get one from Preston."

Bruce escorts Craig back to his van and I follow Nadine to the cruiser. Once we're seated in the cruiser's front seats, she pulls out a notebook and pen from one of her pockets. "First thing, are you injured? Do you need any medical attention?"

"No, I'm fine. Just a little shaken up."

"I don't blame you. So, tell me what happened."

"I had our latest supply of cannabis in bags in the back of the truck. I was taking them to Green Fields in Brantford. I noticed a big black SUV following close behind me."

"How long was this vehicle following you?"

I hesitate before answering. "Umm, I'm not sure. I only noticed them right before they forced me to pull over."

"Did you make out the make, model, age and plate number of the vehicle?"

"It was a Yukon. Like I said, it was black. A year or two old. Sorry, I was so nervous I forget to look at the plates."

"Gotcha. Which Yukon model was it; the standard or XL?"

"No clue."

She pauses her questioning while she jots down my response in her notebook. "How did they force you off the road?"

"They signalled to pass and pulled over to the other side of the road. I noticed they were driving next to me on my left but not passing. When I looked over, the passenger in the front was leaning out of his open window with a gun pointed at me. He signaled with his other hand to pull over." I raise my left arm to demonstrate.

"Jesus Murphy!" Nadine cries as she looks up from her notebook. "How many were there?"

"Two guys."

"Can you describe what they looked like? And what they were wearing?"

"They were wearing masks. You know, those Guy Fawkes masks?"

"Like in the movie *V for Vendetta*?"

"Yeah. They were sort of dressed the same – black pants and jackets. Not sure about heights but maybe anywhere from five-foot, nine to over six feet tall."

"Were they white, black, young looking, any distinguishing features like tattoos? Did any of them talk to you? Did they have accents? Was there anything that stands out?"

I take a deep breath before responding. "They were definitely white guys. I couldn't tell what age they were because they were wearing masks. Only one of them spoke. He had no accent. Spoke like anyone else around here."

"How do you know he's from around here?"

"I don't. Nadine, that's just an expression."

"I thought maybe you subconsciously recognized his voice."

"Look, I'm positive I didn't recognize the voice."

"Gotcha. What else can you tell me about the perpetrators?"

"Umm, not much more," I say, rubbing the back of my neck. "Sorry, it's all a jumble right now."

"Things may come back to you over time. That's what we were taught in police school. You can always provide more details later. What about guns?"

"I only saw the one, pointed at my head. It was a black pistol. My guess is an automatic or semi-automatic nine-millimeter," I say, shaking my head. "I'm not sure of the make. I'm more familiar with hunting rifles."

"So, the other guy didn't have a gun?"

"I didn't see another gun."

"But there could have been another gun?"

"Yeah, there might have been," I say, clenching my jaw. "Nadine, where is this going?"

"Hey, I'm only trying to get the facts straight while they're fresh in your mind. What happened next?"

"One guy pushed me to the ground, face down. After that, I didn't see much. He bound my hands behind my back and my ankles using duct tape."

"Was it the guy holding the gun?"

"Yeah, it was."

"What did he do with the gun? Did he put it in his pocket? Or did he hand it to his buddy?"

"I don't know."

"Really? I would have been mindful of a gun pointed at me. It seems you weren't paying attention to much of anything. Are you sure there was even two guys?"

I let out a sigh. "I was face down on the ground and couldn't see them. I'm telling you what I remember. If you're going to ask whether they were wearing Florsheim or Johnston and Murphy shoes, I have no clue."

"Hey, don't get snarky. I'm only doing my job. So, what happened when you were on the ground? That is, what you were able to see from your vantage point."

"They grabbed the bags of cannabis and threw me into the back of the truck. It was literally all over in minutes."

"How did Craig know to stop and look in the back of the truck?"

"He didn't. I couldn't get my hands or legs free, but I was able to use my feet to get the back door open. After rolling out of the truck, I rolled to the side of the road and tried to signal passing cars until he saw me and stopped."

"Would you be able to demonstrate how you opened the door with your feet?"

"Yeah, but why does it matter?"

"It speaks to the credibility of your story."

"What the fuck, Nadine. Are you telling me you don't believe me?"

"Take it easy, Preston. In police school they taught us to question everything. That's what I'm doing." I can't believe this woman graduated from police school. Ferg is right. These two aren't going to be a problem.

Bruce returns to the cruiser, and Craig drives away in his van. Nadine lowers her window, and Bruce pokes his head inside. "I got his statement."

Nadine nods her head. "These guys sound like pros." She turns back to me. "Any idea how they knew you were going to be delivering the shipment?"

"Nope."

Nadine stops writing and taps her pen on the steering wheel. "You know, this could be an inside job."

"Do you think so?" I ask. "I can't see any of my staff involved in this."

Nadine shrugs her shoulders. "Heck, you never know. Someone has financial problems and gets greedy. Bruce, we're going to have to go to the farm and interview all the employees."

I look back and forth between the two police officers. I didn't expect this. Do I want the police talking to Henry? God knows what he might say to them. "Do you think it's necessary? It doesn't seem like any of them are capable of this."

"You never know," says Bruce. "We gotta check out every possible angle. This, here, is a serious crime for Norfolk."

"Yeah, we better report back to Ferg," says Nadine. "Preston, we need to dust the truck for prints, so it can't be moved until we're done. We also gotta check for any other evidence at the crime scene. They also taught us that at police school."

"I can see they taught some great stuff at police school, but I doubt you'll find any prints other than mine. The robbers wore gloves."

"It's weird that you noticed they wore gloves but don't remember much of anything else," says Nadine as she looks toward her partner, rolling her eyes.

"We still gotta check," responds Bruce. "We'll arrange to get you home."

On the drive to the farm, I lean back in the rear of the cruiser, feeling more comfortable. The two cops appear to have bought the story and not likely to come up with anything. I'm not thrilled about having them interview staff, but glad I decided to pay hush money to Henry. He had better keep his mouth shut or I'm screwed.

CHAPTER 33

I reach for the joint sitting in my ashtray and take a drag. Lately, I've been smoking some weed to help me relax. I continue counting the stack of U.S. hundred-dollar bills on my desk. The door chimes, and I quickly return the money to my safe. After shutting the door, I give the dial a spin to lock it. I've been trying to distract myself by going over paperwork. I'm not regretting the staged robbery, but the two cops investigating it are causing me too much anxiety. My stomach is in revolt and my antacid tablets aren't helping anymore. I plod to the front door where I find Bruce Greening. Around the corner, Nadine Stutz is talking to Bess.

Nadine looks up at me as she rubs Bess' hide. "You got yourself one sweet looking animal here."

"Thanks. She's the family pet," I call out as I go down the steps toward them. "Bess, why don't you say hello to Office Stutz?" Bess nods her head and pounds a hoof on the ground. "That's a good girl."

I usher Nadine and Bruce into the house and direct them into the living room. "So, what did you find out?"

They sit down on one of our couches and I plop down in the one opposite theirs. "Not much of anything," says Nadine, pulling out her notepad and flipping through the pages. "Not that we expected to, but we need to check off all the boxes. That's what they taught us in police school."

Every time she mentions police school, I have to keep myself from laughing. Is she that dumb or is this an act? No leads from the staff have me relieved but also not surprised. My main concern is that these two would start snooping around the old barn.

"So, there's no possibility that someone inside helped the robbers?" I ask.

"We can't be certain," says Bruce. "One of your workers gave off weird vibes."

The comment makes the hair on the back of my neck stand up. "Who?"

"A guy named Henry," says Bruce.

I feel my skin go clammy. "Umm, what did he say?"

"Nothing helpful," says Bruce shrugging his shoulders. "It felt like he was hiding something. Doing this work, you get a sixth sense. I'd keep my eye on that guy."

I exhale and lean back in my seat. "Yeah, I'll do that."

"I suggest that you also tighten up your security measures," offers Nadine. "This is your second robbery, and this one appears to be much better planned than that smash and grab last year."

She continues to flip through her notes. "Now, you had a contractor here fixing up your barn."

The muscles in my neck tighten. "Yeah."

"Any chance that one of them might have been working with the robbers?"

I look off in the distance as if deep in thought. "Hmm, I can't see how they would know anything about our shipments. They haven't been here in months."

"Yeah, that's kinda what we thought too," says Bruce. "But we gotta check off all the boxes."

I can't help from rolling my eyes. These two are like stereotypes in a movie about small town cops. What am I so uptight about? They'd have problems confirming gender in a nudist colony. "Is there anything else I can help you with?"

Nadine pulls at the hair elastic that holds her short ponytail together. "I don't think so, unless there's someone who we haven't interviewed yet."

"Good Lord! The police are here!"

We turn toward the door to the hallway where Mum is standing, rubbing her hands together and grinning. Jesus Murphy. I need to get Mum out of here somehow.

"Good afternoon, Mrs. McPherson," says Nadine.

"You've finally come to investigate all the criminal activity taking place here," she says.

The police officers look at each other, not sure how to react.

I let out a sigh and shake my head. "Mum, can I get you something?"

Nadine puts up her hand. "Hang on, we haven't interviewed your mom yet. Mrs. McPherson, why don't you elaborate on all the criminal activity you've been seeing?"

"I would love to," she says, dropping into a chair. "I've spoken to your sergeant on many occasions, but he doesn't take me seriously. At times, I'm so frightened, I've contemplated sleeping with a gun under my pillow."

Nadine gets her pen and worn-out notebook ready to take down all the sordid details. I sit back and say nothing. There's no point.

"Ever since this smarmy Jimmy character shows up here, strange things have been happening. I know this guy is a mobster. He's been threatening and intimidating my family. If my late husband were still alive, he would know how to deal with him. But my poor Preston is way over his head."

"Can you be more specific, Mrs. McPherson?" asks Bruce. "What types of things has this Jimmy fellow done?"

"For one thing, they took away all of our cows. This is now the most pathetic dairy farm in the county. He waltzes in here every so often like he owns the place. There are all these suspicious workers that I've never seen before. I think Jimmy has sent them over. God knows what they're doing because it's not like there's cows to milk. The farm is a sham now for some criminal enterprise."

Nadine turns to me. "You never mentioned anyone named Jimmy."

"Jimmy Scarpini is a rep from Green Fields, the cannabis company I'm in partnership with. You know, the company we were delivering the marijuana to when I was robbed."

Nadine puts away her notebook again. "Oh."

"Preston is covering up for him," Mum says as her face turns red. "The entire family cowers in fear. I would do something about it but I'm an old woman. I suspect drugs are involved. I recently saw a TV documentary called *Breaking Bad* that was about how drugs are distributed."

"Mum, *Breaking Bad* isn't a documentary. It's a fictional TV series."

Nadine nudges her partner and stands up. "I think we're done here. Thanks for the information, Mrs. McPherson. Preston. We'll be in touch."

Once the police cruiser leaves the property, I fish my phone out from my pocket to call Ferg. After a couple of rings, he answers. "Hey, Mac, what's up?"

"Nadine and Bruce came by again."

"Was there a problem?"

"Yeah, they're starting to make me nervous. Can't you get them to finish their stupid investigation?"

"Stop worrying. They are only doing their job and don't suspect a thing. What will make people suspicious is if I interfere in an investigation involving family. Just play it cool."

"You'll tell me if I have something to worry about, right?"

"Yeah. Yeah. I got your back, Mac."

CHAPTER 34

Ferg was right about Nadine and Bruce. They run out of people to interview, and the interviews they conducted lead nowhere. There are no witnesses. They aren't able to trace the vehicle allegedly involved in the robbery without plates. Green Fields decides that they will pick up our cannabis shipments and provide security while in transit. That satisfies our insurance carrier after I make a second claim in two years. I didn't want to file a claim, but not submitting one would have looked suspicious. The insurer was satisfied with the police report on the robbery and didn't bother sending their own investigators. So, I end up selling the "stolen" weed to Ramone and get reimbursed for the loss from our insurer. On paper we still look like we're only getting by, but in reality, I'm flush with cash. I don't feel nearly as uneasy, and my anxiety levels have settled down. Maybe this is going to work out after all.

While waiting for Guy to show up for another cash exchange, I kill time by doing paperwork in my office and smoking some weed. The door chimes and I check the time. It's well before Guy's appointment and he's never early. When I yank open the door, I find Henry staring at me with a smirk on his face.

"What are you doing here? It's not the end of the month."

"Aren't you going to invite me in?"

My instincts tell me to slam the door in this weasel's face. I fucking hate his guts. Finally, I step aside, and he strolls in. "Now what do you want?"

He slides his hands in his pockets and looks down at the floor. "You know last month when the police interviewed all us workers about your robbery?"

"Yeah, what about it?"

"I didn't say nothing. But I could have."

Anger and anxiety are quickly building. I feel my face flush, and my stomach is in knots. "Am I supposed to thank you or something?"

"I was thinking that I deserve a raise," he says sneering like a cat on the hunt.

"Is that so? If I don't give you a raise, what are you going do? Talk to the police?"

"Yeah. I might remember stuff I forgot to mention the last time."

"So, you would be willing to lose the thousand dollars a week."

"I think you got more to lose than me."

I sigh and smile at his amateurish ploy. "Hang on. I'll be right back."

I creep back to my office and open one of the desk drawers. Reaching to the bottom of the drawer, I pull out a revolver and slip it into my waistband. When I return to the front entrance, he's still there with his hands shoved into his pockets. As I get closer, I pull out the revolver and point it at his stupid face. "This is what I think of your proposal."

Henry steps back with his hands in the air. "You're bluffing."

"You think so?" I ask, my voice quickly rising. "You think I wouldn't love to get rid of a problem employee who keeps coming around trying to blackmail me? Give me a reason why I shouldn't pull this trigger, because my finger has got a real itch."

The smirk is gone now and replaced with a glazed look. His body trembles, and his back is up against the door when he runs out of space to backpedal. "You ain't going to get away with it. Fucking put that gun down."

A wave of heat fills my face, and my finger begins to gently apply more pressure on the trigger. No one is around right now. *Who would know?*

"Okay...okay," he sputters, tears streaking his cheeks. "I'm not going to say anything. Now let me go."

I drop the gun to my side and grab him by the collar. "You can go. And I'll keep to our original arrangement because I'm a fair guy. But try this stunt again and you'll be planted somewhere on this farm, never to be seen or heard from again. Is that clear?"

I release my grip on him, and he turns to fling open the door. As he stumbles down the steps, he trips and falls to the ground. He frantically gets back on his feet and scampers back to the greenhouses.

***

After Henry leaves, I'm too agitated to return to my paperwork. Once I've put away my gun, I stand at the living room window staring out at the roadway in front of the house. I'm not sure how long I've been standing in front of the window when a white Lexus pulls up to the front of the house. Guy gets out of the car and walks toward our front door with his beat-up briefcase tucked under his arm. I swing open the door and he walks in, heading straight through to the kitchen. He places his briefcase on the table, flipping it open. I don't even bother to offer him a drink. I want to get this over with as quickly as possible.

"Where's yer missis?"

"She's out." I don't want to mention that we've split up. The less he knows about my personal life, the better.

"Owt shoppin'? Sayms loike 'er's always owt shoppin' mayte. It's bostin' yow got this cash comin' regular loike. Yow goo-in ter nayd it." He laughs at his own joke, which only brings on a pained look for me. Half the time I have no clue what he's saying with that Brummie accent of his.

I get from my office several large stacks of American hundred-dollar bills and place them on the kitchen table next to the briefcase. "That's one hundred and twenty thousand dollars."

He pulls out an equivalent amount of Canadian bills from the briefcase and replaces them with the U.S. funds. "The exchaynge rayte ta-day is wun dollur an' thirty-wun point foive cents plus me commission." He pushes the money across the table.

Two minutes later, I escort him to his car. As he's getting in, he turns to me. "What am yow burnin' over there?" he asks, pointing at the west side of the farm. "Smells a bit loike whacky-tabaccy."

I turn to the direction he's pointing at where there's a large plume of smoke rising from the direction of the renovated barn. "Oh fuck!"

I grab my keys and tear up the roadway in my car. As I approach, the barn is engulfed in flames that leap high into the sky. Even before I open the car door, I can feel the intense heat given off by the inferno. Pulling up next to my car are Sara and Habib. The three of us stand silently for some time, mesmerized by the blaze, much like I did as a kid when we lit a bonfire. Sara is sobbing loudly. Finally, I let out a scream. A scream that could be heard throughout the county. A scream that expressed my anger, frustration, and despair. Part of me wants to run into the burning structure and end it all. The other two look at me with shocked expression. I slump to the ground, holding my head.

Still crying, Sara drops down on her knees and hugs me. "Are you alright?"

I have no answer for her. I don't really know.

The flames lick at the dry timber, hissing and cracking as the fire consumes everything in its path. Habib breaks the silence. "You want I should call the fire department?"

Do I really want the fire department to know what we've been doing here? There's no point. The barn can't be saved, and it's not like the fire can spread anywhere. I shake my head.

Sara grabs my arm and pulls me up onto my feet. "Dad, let's go. Nothing we can do now."

***

We sit grimly around the dining room table. No one says anything. Sara's eyes are red from crying. I'm obsessively stirring my coffee. My spoon clinking on the side of the mug is the only sound in the room. I hear the front door open. Neither of us bother to get up to see who it is.

"Jesus Murphy, this place looks like a funeral home," declares Ferg as he tiptoes into the room.

"Uncle Ferg, your analogy is quite appropriate considering what those Michigan dealers might do when we can't deliver on our next shipment," replies Sara.

"Whenever things begin to be going well," I say, staring at the wall in front me, "something else blows up on us."

"This is a farm family," declares Ferg. "You're accustomed to dealing with adversity and setbacks. You're the one that always says how you deal with weather, pestilence, economic downturns, and bad politics. You can even rebuild that barn. Anything is possible."

"Is it possible to rebuild it before a week from next Wednesday when our next shipment to Michigan is due? So, don't tell me anything is possible."

Ferg grabs a seat next to me and looks me in the eyes. "You don't need to rebuild the grow-op by Wednesday. You only need to come up with a supply of weed for Ramone. That's more doable."

I shake my head. "We had two supplies of weed and one is now gone. The remaining supply can't meet the needs of both Ramone and Green Fields."

"I get that," says Ferg. "Where else can we get hold of some weed for you?"

"How much seized weed is the OPP holding?" I ask.

Ferg frowns and waves a hand in my face. "That's not happening. I'd never get away with stealing evidence. Grabbing a half ounce is one thing. Heisting one hundred pounds is out of the question."

"What do you expect me to do? Hijack a weed shipment? Wait a minute...," I get up from the table and pace around the room.

Sara's eyes follow me as I dart back and forth across the room. "You're not considering hijacking another one of our shipments, are you?"

I come to a sudden stop. "Of course not. But it's no secret that there are illegal grow-ops in the area. That's where the seized weed comes from. Isn't that so, Ferg?"

"Yeah. What are you getting at?"

"Why don't we steal some weed from one of these illegal growers? It's not like they're going to report it to the police."

"Dad, that's a crazy idea," says Sara. "We have no idea where these grow-ops are. Even if we did, you have no idea what you would be getting yourself into and how dangerous it would be."

I lean my forehead up against one of the walls with my eyes clenched shut. "We need to come up with some solution."

"Besides, even if you were to pull it off, how will a theft resolve our situation?" asks Sara. "Sure, you'll make this month's delivery. But what are you going to do next month?"

"I don't know yet. Let's deal with the next shipment for now."

"You know your daughter is talking sense," says Ferg. "Even I think this is nuts."

I spin around toward Ferg. "Do you know of any illegal grow-ops within a two-hour drive?"

"I think I can come up with some locations."

"Dad, this is some scary shit. There must be another way."

"Like what? Buy weed on the legal market? You can only buy an ounce at a time. We need a hundred pounds."

"Okay, I'll help anyway I can," says Ferg hesitantly.

"Great, because you're going to pull this off with me. You know the two guys who hijacked our Green Fields shipment?" The other two look at me, unsure at what I'm getting at. "The two guys wearing the Guy Fawkes masks. They're going to hold up the grow-op."

"There's no way we're going to hijack a grow-op shipment," says Ferg.

"That's right," I reply. "But we can bust into a greenhouse at night and swipe enough weed to hold me for another month."

"I hate the idea," says Sara, with a look of resignation. "But I suppose it beats being shot by a couple of gangsters."

CHAPTER 35

Ferg did find out about an illegal marijuana operation. It's not exactly as simple as googling illegal grow-ops in Norfolk County, but Ferg heard about one that the OPP drug squad had caught wind of. This farm is northwest of us in a secluded area. Good place to be growing illegally, but also not the easiest place to find. Eventually, Ferg comes up with an address.

On the night of our planned heist, Ferg meets me at the house. "I'll drive," I say, getting behind the wheel of the truck. "You can navigate."

"You ain't stoned, are you?"

"No, but why should that matter?"

"Because I need you totally focused on what we need to do tonight," says Ferg. "I noticed you've been smoking a lot of dope lately."

"That's horseshit and also none of your business."

The truck rumbles down the highway heading north for about thirty minutes. The sun is low in the horizon and, combined with heavy cloud cover, the landscape takes on a grayish tone. "When do I turn off?" I ask.

Ferg doesn't answer.

"Can you get off Facebook and navigate?"

"I'll let you know when it's time to turn off."

I switch on the radio to find some decent music. Anything to provide a distraction and calm my nerves. I know this can go horribly wrong. But, on the other hand, if we pull it off, it buys us some more time. Right now, time is what we need to come up with a better plan.

"About a quarter mile, turn left," says Ferg.

"Left? Are you sure? This area looks more like forest than farmland."

"I'm only passing on the directions Google is giving me."

Less than a minute later, I turn onto a dirt road. "It's about two miles up ahead," says Ferg.

I shut off the radio and concentrate on the landscape. My eyes have difficulty adjusting to the lighting as we pass in and out of shadows cast by the trees lining the roadway.

"Slow down," says Ferg. "It should be right after that bend in the road."

I ease up on the gas until we reach a fenced property. There's a weather-worn sign next to a gate that reads Donsky's Flower Nursery.

"Jesus Murphy, this is a nursery," I say, not even trying to hide my annoyance.

"Do you expect them to put up a sign that says Marty's Illegal Marijuana Grow-op? I'm sure this is the place."

I shut off the truck, and Ferg hands me a mask. My stomach has a massive knot that is working its way up my throat. I can barely speak. I pull out a bottle of antacid tablets from my pocket and swallow three. From the back of the truck, I pull out green trash bags, flashlights, some tools, and rolls of duct tape. I go back to the driver's compartment and reach down under the seats to pull out a couple of handguns. Ferg grabs one and tucks it under his belt. He hands the other one to me. We pull the masks over our faces.

"Let's head straight to the greenhouses," whispers Ferg, opening the gate. "If we run into anyone, let me do the talking."

I nod my head and follow him onto the property. We creep along a gravel road for about four hundred yards until we spot a set of greenhouses in the distance. Ferg turns to me and points in their direction. I nod. The only sound is our boots crunching against the gravel under us. There doesn't appear to be anyone on the property.

We arrive at the greenhouse after a several minutes. Ferg signals that I go inside while he keeps a lookout outside. I give him the okay sign and try to push the greenhouse door open. It's locked.

Ferg whispers in my ear. "See the speaker over the door?" I nod. "That's the speaker for the alarm system. Cut the wire to the speaker and any coaxial cable line going into the greenhouse. That should disable the security system."

After cutting all the lines that I can find, I put down my flashlight and use a crowbar to force the door open. I'm surprised that the greenhouse is in darkness since marijuana plants need lots of light. I pick up the flashlight and turn it on. As I walk down the aisles with my light, I discover it's full of flowers. Not a single marijuana plant. *Just flowers.*

I stumble out of the greenhouse and grab Ferg by the collars of his jacket. "You fucking idiot. This is an actual flower nursery."

"Shhh. Check that greenhouse over there," he says, pointing to the structure to the right.

I scoot over to the next greenhouse. After disabling the security, I force the door open and poke my head inside. Scanning the building with my flashlight, I again see wall-to-wall flowers. I turn around and race back to Ferg. "Let's get out of here."

Ten minutes later, we're back in the truck. "Explain to me how come we ended up at a nursery?" I ask, trying to stay calm. "Let me guess. Your reliable source was wrong."

Ferg is busy looking at his phone and ignores me.

"Are you even listening to me?"

He looks up from his phone. "I heard you, Mac. The problem is that I googled the wrong address."

"That's just great," I say, shaking my head. "That's like saying I know there's a bank in town and end up at the address of the post office."

Ferg is still focused on his phone. "Shut up and turn the truck around. The grow-op is about ten minutes away."

"Are you sure?"

"Just drive."

I gun the engine and execute a three-point turn, heading back in the direction we came from. Once we arrive back at the main road, Ferg instructs me to make a left turn. It seems the grow-op is on fifteenth Concession Road, not fourteenth. When we reach the location of the alleged grow-op, there's no sign outside the property but there is a locked gate and high fencing. I pull out a toolbox from the truck and fish out a set of wire cutters. That gets us past the main gate.

We silently creep along the main road. I can here dogs barking somewhere on the property. They sound like big dogs. Condensation is collecting under my Guy Fawkes mask and dripping down my face. This time it's easy to find the greenhouses because, as expected, they're lit up. This must be the right place. I tread gently, trying my best to not make a sound. As we get closer, we try to avoid the lights and stay in the shadows. About one hundred feet from the first greenhouse, we stop and crouch behind several trees.

Ferg points to a figure walking outside the greenhouse. He seems to be alone. "I'm going to make my way to the back of the greenhouse and surprise him," he says barely whispering. "You stay here until I'm on him."

"How do we know there isn't anyone else?"

"We'll deal with that when it comes up."

"Gotcha. Let's do it."

Ferg disappears into the darkness, and I watch the person outside the greenhouse. He's loading plants onto a trailer hitched to a tractor. Several minutes pass and no sign of Ferg. Then the person loading the plants freezes. Out of the shadows appears Ferg with a gun at the guy's head. I rush towards them. By the time I reach them, Ferg has him on the ground lying on his stomach. Ferg holds a finger up to his lips.

I stoop down and wrap duct tape around his wrists and ankles.

"Who the fuck are..." the rest is inaudible because Ferg stuffs a rag in his mouth and holds it in place with duct tape.

Ferg signals toward the greenhouse. I look inside but quickly return. None of these plants are flowering. There's no point in taking plants that need maturing. The other greenhouses are locked. While Ferg watches for employees, I search for security system cables. I cut all the wiring I can find and pry the doors open. In the fourth greenhouse, I discover the room is full of flowering plants.

Ferg sticks his head into the greenhouse. "Turn off your light. I think there's someone else walking around." I give him a thumbs up.

I've brought along a cutting took and snip off ripe buds and toss them into a bag. Moving as quickly as I can, I fill two bags and work on a third one.

A voice booms across the greenhouse. "What's going on here?"

I wheel around to find a shotgun and a flashlight trained on me. I drop the cutting tool and my bag and slowly raise my arms over my head. The guy holding the gun isn't even thirty years old with sandy brown hair and a beard.

"Who are you?" he demands.

I say nothing.

He puts down the light and pulls out his phone, dialing a number. "You need to come out right away to the greenhouses."

I take a couple of steps toward him, trying to maintain his attention. Right behind him, close to the entrance, Ferg is quietly moving toward us.

"Hey, stay where you are unless you want me to blow your fucking head off," he says.

I move toward him, which is obviously making him nervous because the shotgun barrel is shaky in his grip.

"I'll take that gun, thanks," says Ferg who has his own gun against the man's temple. He gently pulls the shotgun out of his hands. "And your phone. Now get down on the floor face first."

The guy slowly drops to the floor. "You guys are dead men."

"Shut up," barks Ferg.

While Ferg gags him and ties up his feet and hands with duct tape, I pick up the cutting tool and rush to fill my bags with buds while Ferg stands guard outside.

When I'm done, I drag a couple of bags outside and hand them to Ferg. When I return with the rest of the bags, we head back in the direction of the truck. The dogs have begun barking again, and the barking is getting louder. I break out into a sprint. "Move it, Ferg! They've let the dogs loose."

As I slow down, a shot is fired. That gets the adrenaline to kick in. When we reach the gate, I slam it shut and jam a stick in the gate latch to keep it from opening at the same time three rottweilers arrive. The dogs have a crazed look in their eyes as they try to jump over the gate. I stumble over to the truck to help Ferg load all the bags and everything else we've brought with us into the back. I toss my mask and gloves in and slam the back door shut. I dive into the driver's seat and Ferg flies into the passenger side. My heart is pounding, and I can barely breathe as I fumble with the keys to start the truck. As the engine comes alive, we duck at the sound of an explosion. My side-view mirror is gone.

"Get the fuck out of here now!" screams Ferg in between gasps for air. I lean into the accelerator as two more shots are fired. We disappear into the night.

CHAPTER 36

It's quite late when I get home. I have trouble falling asleep but eventually drift off. I dream I'm back behind the wheel of the truck with Ferg.

"How much weed do you think you've been able to nab?" asks Ferg.

"I wasn't doing a neat job clipping the flowers. Once we dry and trim the heads, the four bags should produce between seventy-five and a hundred pounds of weed. I ran through the greenhouse so fast I don't even know what strains I picked up."

"The bags sure felt heavy."

I look in my rear-view mirror and notice a set of headlights quickly approaching. "Ferg, I may be a little paranoid, but I think they could be following us."

He turns around in his seat to look out the back window. "How long have you noticed them?"

"I don't know. A couple of minutes."

"You better get this thing moving."

I speed up but the car behind us keeps closing the gap. Then I hear the blast of a shotgun.

"It's definitely them," says Ferg. He's got his revolver out on his lap. "Can't you go any faster?"

"This is a truck, not a racing car. I'm not going to be able to out-run them," I say. Then Ferg pulls his gun out. "What are you planning to do? Get into a shootout with them?"

"I'm not going make it easy for them."

The car crosses the to the other side of the road and pulls up next to us. When it begins to nudge its way in into our lane, I realize they are trying to force us off the road. "We're going to get killed if I don't stop!"

Ferg has his gun raised, trying to aim at the driver. He fires his weapon, and the bullet shatters glass but doesn't appear to hit anyone.

"You're crazy!" I scream, sweat pouring down my face.

A gunshot echoes across the deserted highway, and the steering wheel pulls to one side. They've blown out a tire. I struggle to control the truck as I pull over to the shoulder. The SUV pulls up in front of us, and four guys scramble out with weapons pointed at us. I look over at Ferg. "Don't do anything stupid."

"Get out of the truck with your hands up," *orders one of them.*

I slowly open my door and step out with my hands raised. I look over to my right, and Ferg has done the same. A guy with a long bushy beard and a shaved head walks over to the truck and grabs Ferg's gun off the front seat. He glares at us as he spits in our direction. "You two fucking pieces of shit are going to pay for this."

He turns to one of his cronies. "Check them for ID." *He keeps is gun pointed at us as the other guy pulls our wallets out of our pockets.*

Flipping open our wallets, his jaw drops. "This one here is a cop," *he says, pointing at Ferg.*

The other two guys trot over to look. "Shit!" *says one of them.* "What are we going to do now?"

The guy with the beard grins and walks right over to Ferg until he's inches from his face. "I wouldn't be too worried about a dirty cop."

"Maybe we can, umm, negotiate a deal," *I say, my voice quivering.*

All four of them laugh. "Dude, do you expect me to buy my own weed back?" *asks the bearded guy, his lips curled.*

"No. No. I'll give you one hundred thousand dollars if you let us go."

"You got that much money on you?"

"Umm, no."

"What are you going to do?" *he cackles.* "You gonna write me a cheque?" *His crew break out in laughter again.*

"I can get it for you."

"Sure, I'm going to let you two fuckers go, and we'll kinda meet up for coffee later in the week to settle up." *He raises his gun to my temple.* "How fucking stupid do I look?"

"Let him go and you can hold me until he's back with the money," *blurts out Ferg.*

"I don't want your money, and neither of you motherfuckers are going anywhere." *He shoves me down onto my knees. One of the other guys does the same to Ferg.*

"You kill me, and half the OPP will be crawling all over the county," *says Ferg.* "Your grow-op will be one of the first places they'll look."

"Shut the fuck up!" someone behind me yells. I feel the barrel of a gun pressed against my head. "One...two..."

"Please don't." Tears are streaming down my face.

"Three..."

My head jerks up, and I'm drenched in sweat. The alarm displays 4:37 a.m. I've barely got an hour of sleep.

I swing around my legs off the bed and feel around for my slippers with my feet. After sliding into them, I quietly get up and trudge down the hall to the kitchen. I switch on the lights under the cabinets and reach for a glass in the drying rack next to the sink. After pouring myself some water, I sit down at the kitchen table. In front of me is an ashtray with a partially smoked joint. I pick it up and look for my lighter.

***

Yesterday I made our latest delivery to Ramone's people with the weed stolen from the grow-op. In hindsight, the robbery was madness. I might have been shot or killed. I can't do this again. I'm fortunate no one ever noticed the barn fire. The smoke was visible for miles, but no one mentioned anything.

I decide to set up a meeting with Ramone. I need to find a way to end our relationship before something terrible happens.

My morning is uneventful. Along with a couple of employees, I spend a few hours trimming mother plants. As we wrap up, Jake wheels a trolley with the cutting waste out of the greenhouse. "I'm heading to the house for a bite to eat," I call out to Jake before heading out the door. "I'll be back to finish later."

"Sure thing, Mr. McPherson."

As my truck rumbles down the roadway to the house, I spot a police cruiser parked out front. Inside the house, Nadine and Bruce are seated in our living room chatting with Sara.

I feel a huge lump form in my gut. I take a deep breath, hoping to slow down my heart. "What brings you folks here?"

"We were telling your daughter that we may have gotten a breakthrough on the truck hijacking," says Bruce.

My chest tightens. "Oh really?" I drop down into a seat and glance over to Sara. It seems like every muscle in her face has tightened.

"A couple of interesting developments occurred recently that might be related to your robbery," says Nadine.

"What do you mean?" I ask.

Nadine pulls out her notepad and flips through it. "Word on the street is that an illegal grow-op near Clarke Summit was robbed. We've been watching this place for a while and were planning to bust them. Anyway, the heist may have been carried out by the same guys that robbed you."

"You're kidding," I remark, gripping a pillow on the couch. "I hear a lot of illegal farms are getting hit. Did you visit the grow-op?"

"We did," says Bruce. "But they're not admitting to anything."

"So, you don't know anymore than you did before?" asks Sara.

"This might be a coincidence," adds Bruce with a raised eyebrow, "but it just so happens that another break in occurred that same evening, although nothing was stolen."

"Another grow-op?"

"No. It was a flower nursery," says Bruce.

I tense up so much that I find it difficult to breathe properly. "Why would you think that the two events are related?"

"We're trying to connect the dots actually," responds Nadine. "That's something they taught us in police school. It may not mean anything, but we're trying to figure out if there's a connection. What if they robbers were confused and showed up at the wrong farm? They break into the greenhouses and find flowers instead of cannabis. So, they leave without stealing anything only to show up later at the grow-op a few miles away."

I force a small smile and attempt to patronize Nadine. "Sounds like you learned a heck of a lot in police school. But why do you think these events are related to our robbery?"

"These fellas were wearing Guy Fawkes masks, like in the movie *V for Vendetta*," she says pulling her phone out of her jackets.

"How do you know that? You said the grow-op people weren't talking."

"That's true," she says. "These guys were smart enough to cut lines to security systems, but one of the security cameras at the nursery was missed and picked some images of the guys who broke into the greenhouses. This is all too much of a coincidence. Guys with mask rob you. Guys with the same masks break into a nursery. Then, on the same day, a grow-op in the same area is allegedly robbed."

Nadine plays a video on her phone of two men in masks running away from a greenhouse. It's a grainy black and white image that I try to convince myself they the suspects looks nothing like Ferg and me. There must have been surveillance cameras that we missed.

"Do these guys look familiar?"

I stare at the screen, trying not to show any emotions. "Hard to make out much. They don't look familiar."

"What I mean is, do they look like the guys who robbed you?"

I shrug. "Could be."

"What do you mean could be? They're even wearing the same masks."

"If you're asking me to make a definitive ID based on this low-quality video, I can't. But it might be the guys. It's likely the guys but I can't confirm it."

I finally look away. We intentionally wanted any evidence to point to our staged robbery but seeing myself on the surveillance video was freaking me out. My heart is pounding, and I feel flushed. If Ferg hadn't googled the wrong address, there wouldn't even be this evidence available to the police.

Sara hasn't said a thing until now. "What does this all mean?"

Bruce leans forward in his seat and speaks in a steady low-pitched voice. "We believe there's a gang working the area robbing cannabis producers. We don't know if they're from the area or have moved in to hit a few places. Other than this video and your dad's description, we don't have much else to go on right now. We have forensic people at the nursery looking for more clues."

I don't like the sound of that. What if they find some evidence? I need to speak to Ferg. "Good luck, and if I think of anything else, I'll be sure to contact you."

The two police officers get up from the couch. "Thanks for your assistance, folks." I walk them to the door. As Nadine steps outside, she stops and turns around. "I noticed that the driver side-view mirror on your truck is broken. It was fine on the day you were held up."

"Umm, yeah. That just happened on the weekend."

Nadine walks over and looks at it more closely. "Interesting how it broke. It doesn't look like it was knocked off but rather it shattered. See how the base has no signs of stress."

"I was on the highway, passing a transport truck when I heard an explosion next to me. I turned and noticed the mirror was gone. My guess is that a big stone was fired from one of the truck's tires and hit my mirror at high speed."

"Hmm, I never seen that before. Though I've seen a lot of shattered windshields. You better get that fixed." Nadine finally returns to the police cruiser and gets into the passenger seat.

I wave as they drive off. As soon as they've left the property, I fish my phone out of my pocket to call Ferg. "Your snoopy cops were here with a video of us at the nursery. What the fuck, Ferg!"

"Relax, Mac. You can't tell who it is in that crappy video."

"You knew about the video and didn't tell me?"

"I'm sorry. I forgot to mention it. There's nothing else but the video."

"I thought this investigation would be over by now. They're like a dog with a bone, especially that Nadine. If you ask me, it doesn't look like she's about to give up."

"Don't worry. I'm on top of this. Everything will be fine."

"What if they find some new evidence at the nursery?"

"We wore gloves, Mac. They aren't even going to find our shoeprints two weeks later among all the other shoeprints left by workers going in and out of the greenhouses."

"Damn it, you better be right."

CHAPTER 37

"Hey, Mac, it's Graham."

"Hi, Graham," I say, cringing at the sound of his voice. "What's up?"

"I wanted to tell you that Dad hasn't been doing well and won't likely be able to make the family meeting coming up in a few weeks."

"Sorry to hear about Uncle Liam. I'll give him a call."

"By the way, I saw your latest numbers and I'm impressed. I always knew cannabis was the right direction for the farm. You must be pleased."

I don't want to deal with this annoying SOB at this moment. If he thinks I'm going to thank him for pushing me out of dairy farming, that ain't going to ever happen. Even if hell freezes over. "I was about to step out, Graham. Thanks for the heads up on Uncle Liam. I will see you at the family meeting."

"Okay, bye. See you then."

I end the call, put away my phone, and grab my keys to head into town. Stepping outside, the warm breeze and sunshine brightens my mood, but only for a moment. Then I recognize two familiar white vans lumbering toward the house. The last people I want to deal with today are those bothersome inspectors.

They pull up next to my car and get out, walking toward me.

"I'm Glen Fleming, an inspector from the Ontario Cannabis Agency."

"And I'm Phil Garneau, an inspector from the federal Department of Health."

They both hand me business cards.

"Come on, guys. I know who you are."

Garneau reads a prepared statement regarding government inspection policy and my legal rights.

"Look, I've got to go," I say, walking to my car. "You know where the greenhouses are. You've met Jake, who should be able to answer most of your questions. My daughter is inside the house and can show you the records."

"Thanks for your cooperation," says Fleming. They return to their vans and drive off to the greenhouses.

On the way to town, I pull out my bottle of antacid tablets. There's only one tablet left in the bottle; that's not going to be enough. I chew it down and toss the bottle out the window. I pass by fields with corn stalks bathing in the morning sun, cows grazing in open meadows, and rows of tobacco almost ready to be picked. Even tobacco isn't as regulated as marijuana. The hypocrites who run the county and annoying women at our church have no problem with growing tobacco. At the outskirts of Delhi, I pull into the parking lot of the OPP satellite office. I tramp into the office and find Ferg behind his desk in front of a stack of papers.

"Hey, Mac. What are you doing here?"

"We need to talk."

He pushes aside the paperwork and motions for me to take a seat across from him. "What's on your mind?"

The office looks like a hurricane has hit the place with paper and file folders scattered on the desk, chairs, cabinets, and even the floor. The furniture is standard government-issue, probably from the 1980s. The garbage bin doesn't look like it's been emptied this month.

I move some files off a chair and sit down. "Nadine and Bruce have got me spooked. They won't let up with their investigation and their endless questions. I feel like it's only a matter of time before these two morons uncover something or I slip up."

"Actually, it's a good thing you dropped by. I've got some more bad news for you." Ferg's voice lowers, and he leans forward in his seat. "It seems that Lucille Lamont and her merry band of protesters mentioned to Nadine and Bruce that she noticed a lot of smoke coming from your farm on the day of the fire. They're talking about checking it out."

The blood drains from my face. "That can't happen!"

"Shhh," whispers Ferg, looking to see if the clerk outside his office reacts to my outburst. "Keep it down. I've told them they got no business investigating rumors coming from stupid Lucille. Besides, they've got more than enough work to do."

I hold my head in my hand. "Shit. Shit. Shit."

"Mac, is there something there that would raise suspicion? After all, it was just a barn fire, right?"

"Maybe," I say rubbing my eyes with my fists. "When the contractor came to look at it, he said the fire was caused by a faulty connection to the main power line. In other words, his fucking fault. I'm not sure if that would be obvious to someone who might be snooping around."

"Mac, you gotta get him to come around and remove anything suspicious."

"This is getting so complicated. I still haven't spoken with Ramone about splitting with him."

"Don't worry, Mac. This will eventually work out. It always does."

I look at him, shaking my head, but not bothering to respond. Then my phone buzzes, and I look down at it. There's a text message from Sara indicating that there's a serious problem with the inspection, and that I need to get back to the farm immediately.

Driving back to the farm, I grip the steering wheel so tight that my knuckles are white. I had forgotten to pick up more pills for my stomach, which feels like it's on fire. When I return to the farm, the inspectors' vans are parked in front of our house. I rush inside past Mum, who is parked in front of the TV, to find the inspectors sitting in my office with Sara, who has a frown pasted on her face.

I grab a seat, trying to show no signs of the panic racing through my body. "What seems to be the problem?"

Garneau glances down at his notes. "Mr. McPherson, there appears to be some serious discrepancies with your records."

"That makes no sense. We've been meticulous with our record-keeping."

"We've double checked everything, and the numbers aren't right," he continues. "We've even found plant strains that don't show up in your inventory."

I flop back into my chair. How can that be? I thought maybe plants from the destroyed barn have been transferred to the other greenhouses, but the barn was using the same mother plants. Did we introduce new strains somehow? Did Henry have something to do with it? Maybe he's sabotaged my operations.

"There must be some logical explanation behind all of this," I say. "I'll look into this and get back to you. We don't have to make a fuss about it."

Garneau shakes his head. "I'm afraid it's not that simple. I'm going to have to recommend to the department that they conduct a review of your producer's license."

"And I'm going to have to recommend that the Ontario Cannabis Agency suspend your provincial sales certification," adds Fleming.

They both get up to leave. "Look I'm sure I can get this straightened out in the next twenty-four hours," I say, following them to the door. "Can't you hold off your reports?"

They continue walking to their vehicles without responding.

CHAPTER 38

Spreadsheets are strewn across by desk. I have spent the past two days desperately trying to make sense of our inventory numbers. Almost two years of doctoring the books to satisfy the government inspectors has finally blown up in my face. I struggle to develop a scenario to explain the inconsistencies that will satisfy the inspectors. So far, I've come up with nothing. We got too sloppy and are now going to pay the price. I come to the conclusion that I'm fucked.

I'm hoping if there's regulatory action taken, it's only a license suspension and they don't revoke our license. I have more than enough money saved to survive a suspension, use the time to clean up our operations, and make a break with Ramone. Then maybe I can return to only legal sales through Green Fields.

My concentration is broken by my chirping phone sitting next to me on my desk. I glance down at it. The call is from Jimmy Scarpini. I wonder if he's heard about the inspection report.

"Good morning, Jimmy."

"Hi, Mac."

"What's up?" As if I don't know why he's calling. I'm sure he's pissed off.

"We got a copy of your last inspection report. What the hell is going on?"

"I know what you must be thinking. The truth is, we've been getting lax here and got sloppy. I'm hoping we only get slapped with a suspension. We're going to use that pause to go over our procedures and clean up everything."

"It's not so simple. You may be in breach of our agreement. Our lawyers are reviewing the report and advising us of our options. Remember, we have a mortgage on the farm, and corporate will want to protect their investment, which appears to be at risk."

"I'm hoping we can work this out somehow."

"I'm on your side for now, but you've upset some important people in the company. This does not look good. We'll be sending auditors over in the next week to go over everything. I expect your full cooperation."

Oh, crap. Now I've got to deal with auditors. They're worse than the cops. The bad news keeps piling up. "Absolutely. I'm so sorry for screwing up. This is our family's farm. We've owned this place for almost a hundred years, and I can't afford to lose it. I'll give you my full cooperation. I hope we can work this out."

"I can't make any promises. I'll keep you informed as best as I can."

"Thanks, Jimmy."

I press the end button and bang my fist on the desktop. I feel like I'm caught in an avalanche and about to get buried alive. Then I remember we have a family meeting coming up next week. The shit is going to hit the fan when Graham and Liam find out about this. I need to buy some time to get us out of this hole.

I look up and see Sara standing at my office door. "Who were you talking to?"

"Green Fields," I say, hanging my head. "Their lawyers are looking at our agreement. It doesn't sound good."

"Oh dear."

Her eyes fill with tears ready to burst. I'm filled with guilt for having betrayed my family.

There's loud pounding coming from the front door. We look at each other, our lined faces revealing concern over who that could be. The banging sound continues as we scamper to see who it is.

I pull the door open and find Ramone standing there in a black suit, wearing his Ray-Ban Aviator sunglasses as usual even though it's an overcast day. Behind him stands his driver and thug, Angel.

"What brings you here?" I decide I want this to be a short conversation, so Sara and I step outside onto the porch instead of inviting them inside. "We were on our way out." We step off the porch onto the gravel driveway.

"I must say I was extremely disappointed in the product you sent us. To be frank, it was crap. I'm not paying nineteen hundred a pound for shitty weed. Ain't that so, Angel?"

Angel nods in agreement. "That's right, boss."

"Where did it come from?" asks Ramone.

"As a matter of fact, umm...I was intending on, umm...talking to you about it," I struggle trying to find the right words. "We had a recent accident and lost a portion of our facilities. And, umm...we won't be able to supply you with anymore product."

Ramone glares at us. "Is that so?"

"I'm terribly sorry but our production has dropped considerably and -"

"Mr. Mac, do I need to remind you we have a business arrangement? And I don't appreciate my partners breaking agreements. Ain't that so, Angel?"

"Not a smart thing to do," says Angel, shaking his head.

Sara grips my arm. "Look, I don't have any to sell to you," I say, trying not to show my dread and anxiety.

Ramone turns in the direction of our greenhouses. "I see lots of weed being grown here. You can provide me with product from there."

"I've already committed to selling that marijuana elsewhere. Well before you came along."

Ramone looks over at Angel and nods his head. Angel pulls out a revolver from his waistband grabs Sara by the arm, pointing the gun at her head. Sara shrieks.

"You wouldn't want something to happen to this nice girl here, would you?" asks Ramone, forcing a smile, revealing his gold grill.

"Put your gun away," I plead, my voice trembling despite trying to remain calm. "You don't understand. The government may be shutting me down."

"So, what?" says Ramone, shaking his head. "You don't need the government to grow. Lots of people do it. You're a smart guy. You'll figure it out."

"But -"

"Or we can take your daughter with us to convince you that we mean business. Is that what you want?"

Angel drags Sara to their SUV by her arm. I dash over to stop him, but before I reach them, I get wacked in the head by Ramone. Everything goes black and I drop to the ground. I hear Ramone talking but I can't make out the words. Then I feel the wind get knocked out of me. I roll over onto my side as another kick connects with my gut.

A loud bang echoes across the property. Seconds later, there's another one.

The beating stops. The only sound is hysterical sobbing from Sara.

Each breath sends spasms of pain shooting through my rib cage. My head throbs as I stumble to my feet and try to focus. I stagger over to a trembling Sara and take her in my arms. Tears stream down her face.

As the fog in my head clears, I look around for Ramone and Angel. Then I realize that Mum is standing in front of us. "Take that, you motherfuckers!" she shouts, pointing a shotgun at the two gangsters lying on the ground. Both have blood pouring out of head wounds.

I teeter over to the bodies and bend down. Neither have a pulse. "Mum, what have you done?"

"I'm protecting my family," she says, frowning. "Someone has to look out for them."

"Holy shit! You've killed them. Like, you've actually killed them."

"You're damn right."

"What are we going to do? We're going to jail for sure now, unless his gangster friends come over from Michigan and kill us first."

I slump down into a sitting position, holding my knees up against my chest. Sara kneels beside me to give me a hug. "We'll think of something. We always do."

I slowly get up and walk to Mum. I yank the gun from her hands. A van tears up the road and stops suddenly in front of us. Habib bolts out of the van. "What happened here?"

I point to the two bodies. "We better call Ferg."

***

Ferg stares at the two bodies sprawled out on the gravel driveway with his hands gripping his belt. "What a friggin' mess." He looks back at me. "How did you ever get two shots off without getting shot yourself?"

"It wasn't me" I say. "It was Mum."

"I keep telling you that there are gangsters threatening my family, and you've done squat about it," says Mum, puffing out her chest. "So, I had to take matters into my own hands."

Habib eyes Mum, keeping his distance. "She makes me nervous."

Ferg bends down to look at the bodies. "Some damn nice shooting, that's for sure."

"I didn't call you over to admire her shooting!" I scream as my face reddens. "What are we going to do with these two?"

Ferg stands up, rubbing his chin. "You've got 350 acres. Let's find somewhere to bury them."

"Here on the property?"

"No one's going to see you digging out on the west end of the property. But you run that risk if you drive the bodies somewhere else. Your biggest worry is if someone decides to come looking for these two."

"I know. Someone must know they were coming here."

"One problem at a time," continues Ferg. "We need a tarp to wrap them up in and some shovels. Looks like we've got a busy day ahead of us."

"Habib, you can get the tarp and shovels," I say. "I'm going to get the tractor and trailer."

"What should I do?" asks Sara.

"You can clean up the blood pooled up on the ground once we remove the bodies," says Ferg. "Get some hydrogen peroxide to pour over the visible spots and then cover them with fresh gravel."

When I return with the tractor, Ramone and Angel are each rolled up in a green tarp. No one says a word. It feels like a dense cloud has descended from above and engulfed us. Sara works to remove the evidence from the driveway. Ferg has changed out of his uniform into some work clothes from inside the house. I climb down from the tractor and walk to one of the wrapped bodies. "I'll pick up this end. Habib, you grab the other."

We bend down and struggle to lift the body. This one must be Angel, who is a big man. Together, we stumble to the trailer hitched to the tractor and strain to push the body onto it. Then we return to load the other one.

Wheezing, I sit on the edge of the trailer to catch my breath. "I'll drive them to the other end of the farm. You two can follow in the truck." Still breathing heavily, I pull myself up to the driver's seat of the tractor and start it up. I rumble to the west end of the farm toward the site of the burned down barn with the truck trailing behind.

Arriving at the site of the old barn, I stop and scan the area. Behind where the barn once stood is a gully which looks like the perfect spot to dig a grave. I get back on the tractor and move it to the edge of the gully. Getting down from the driver's seat, I signal for Ferg and Habib to follow.

"Is anyone going to notice the earth has been dug up here?" asks Ferg.

"Nope," I say. "No one ever comes back this way."

"Then let's start digging."

About a half hour in, I'm wishing I owned a backhoe. Once we dig beyond the topsoil, the ground becomes incredibly hard and compact. It takes two hours to dig deep enough to ensure animals don't uncover the grave.

We drag the bodies over to the hole and drop them in.

"We can't have a murder weapon hanging around your house," says Ferg as he tosses the shotgun into the grave.

"Is it wise to bury it with the bodies?" I ask.

"If two bodies are found on your property, you're pretty much screwed anyway. Besides, no one is going to find this grave."

"Hope not."

After fifteen minutes of throwing the dirt back into the hole, the green tarp is no longer visible. Some of my anxiety begins to dissipate. Another thirty minutes and the hole is filled. We stomp down the earth and trudge back to the vehicles.

"We're half done now," says Ferg. "We have to dump their SUV somewhere."

"Any suggestions?" I ask. "Cleaning up a crime scene isn't our area of expertise."

"Certainly not anywhere in the county. We don't want any connection between them and this farm. Mac, you're going to drive it to Windsor and leave it in a Walmart parking lot. A car with Michigan plates isn't going to stand out in a border city. It'll take days until someone notices it. I'll follow behind in my cruiser."

"I'm so fucking tired. Can't we do this tomorrow?"

"Don't be stupid. We need this out of here now. There can't be any sign of you being in the car, so you're going to wear one of your protective clothing, booties and gloves."

Ferg changes back into his uniform, and I put on the greenhouse protective gear. Before we leave, he hands me a cellphone. "What's this for?" I ask, examining the phone.

"It's a burner phone. Leave yours at home. If you need to make a call, no one will be able to trace it to you."

I slip the phone in my pocket then carefully get into the Escalade and begin the drive to Windsor with Ferg on my tail. The round trip is almost six hours. I wonder, during the trip to Windsor, whether a new black Escalade with Michigan plates being tailed by a police cruiser looks conspicuous. We eventually pull into a Walmart in East Windsor, which is only twenty minutes from the Ambassador Bridge connecting Canada to Detroit. After parking the car, I get out and lock the doors. It's already dusk and, although no one seems to take notice of us, I feel as though there'll be dozens of witnesses coming forward to help the police when the abandoned SUV is discovered. I quickly remove the protective gear and toss them into a bag along with Ramone's key fob. Once back on the highway, we pull off to toss the stuff into a waste bin at a service center.

By the time I arrive home, it's evening. I eat a hot bowl of soup and crash for the night, although it feels like it takes hours to fall asleep. Every cursed thing from the past few weeks returns that night to haunt me – the inspectors, Lucille Lamont, Green Fields, Nadine and Bruce, Ramone.

CHAPTER 39

Ten days after the Ramone's visit, some of the tension around the farm has subsided. None of Ramone's associates show up asking questions about him. Jimmy Scarpini has come around to accept that we bungled our inventory. He has taken up our cause and convinced officials at Green Fields that there was nothing nefarious involved in our inventory mess. They have sent several people to help us sort through our issues. Green Fields lawyers have worked with government officials to mitigate what penalty might be levied on us. There appears to be a light at the end of the tunnel.

I've spoken to our staff and explained that we have some regulatory problems that we are working through and that is why some Green Fields staff are onsite. None of them are aware of the shooting. The sound of a gun being fired is not unusual with Mum around. Even *she* seems less agitated these days.

It's a bright summer day, and the sun is streaming in the greenhouse where I'm supervising plant trimming. Jake and I are chatting when he directs my attention to a figure standing at the greenhouse entrance. "Mr. McPherson, I think Officer Stutz is here to speak to you."

I glance over my shoulder and try not to scowl. Every one of her visits increases my anxiety. I stroll toward her and raise a hand to wave at her. "How's it goin', eh?"

She waits for me at the door to the greenhouse. "There may be a possible new development in your hijacking case."

"What kind of new development?"

"Windsor police report that an abandoned vehicle with Michigan plates was found in a Walmart parking lot. They contacted their counterparts in Detroit who have provided information about the owner. He a known Detroit drug dealer named Ramone Lopez. Detroit police have tried to contact Mr. Lopez with no success. Furthermore, word on the street is that he and an associate, Angel Diaz, have been missing for several weeks."

"How is this related to my robbery?" I ask, furrowing my brows and acting like this is new to me.

"I don't know if it is. Just following a hunch, you know." In her hand is a large brown envelope. She looks inside and pulls out two photos of Ramone and Angel, which she hands over to me. "Do these two guys look familiar?"

I stare at the photos for some time as if it's the first time I've ever seen them. Right now, the police are the least of my worries. I'm still paranoid that some of their Michigan associates will show up here asking questions. Finally, I hand them back. "Never seen them before."

"Could they be the two guys who held you up?"

I shake my head. "I can't tell you one way or the other. Sorry."

"When we compared these photos with the video at the flower nursery, we've concluded that they can't be the same individuals." She holds up her phone and plays the video for me again. "Look - they definitely don't have the same body types as the guys in the video."

"I'm not much of a detective, Nadine. Never been to police school, and I can't make out much of anything in that lousy video."

"It's okay. We're trying to check out every possible lead." Nadine slips the photos back into the envelope and pulls out another one. "You said the hijackers drove a black Yukon. Is that right?"

"Yeah, I'm pretty sure."

"I know you didn't catch the plate number, but you must have noticed whether it had Ontario or Michigan license plates. They're quite different."

Her questions are becoming annoying and making me way too anxious. I'm shifting my weight from one leg to the other, trying to play it cool and wondering how I can get rid of her. "Nadine, I was so scared at the time, I'm surprised I didn't wet my pants. So, excuse me for being short on details."

She hands me the photo she's holding. "Yeah, I get it, Mac. Just trying to put all these pieces together. So, is it possible that it wasn't a Yukon but an Escalade?"

I look down at the photo of Ramone's SUV. I'm not sure what to answer at this point. Maybe the safe answer is to say no. Maybe she's trying to trap me into a scenario where I contradict myself. "No. It was a Yukon." I hand her back the photo.

"So, you're sure it was a Yukon but have no clue if it had Ontario or Michigan plates."

"For fuck sakes! It could have had Chilean plates."

"Gotcha. You didn't notice the plates. Oh, Windsor police are going over the Escalade searching for prints and other forensic evidence. The two missing guys might have been victims of foul play."

I sense she wants to see how I react, but there's nothing to observe. I remain stone-faced and silent. I've underestimated Nadine. She's not so dumb after all. "Is there anything else I can help you with?" I ask.

"That's it. Thanks for your time," she says, turning around to exit the greenhouse. But instead of leaving she stops and spins around. "There is another thing I wanted to ask you."

"I'm awfully busy here but go ahead."

"I hear there was a fire on the property not that long ago."

I feel my face becoming flushed despite my attempts to remain nonchalant. "Oh, yeah. We did have one. What about it?"

"It's normal that folks report a fire. But you didn't."

"That's true, but I didn't see any need to waste anyone's time. It was an old barn that hasn't been used in several decades. It was in such bad shape that if it hadn't burned down, it would have soon fallen down."

"So, you're saying that it wasn't being used."

"That's right."

Nadine pushes back her cap to scratch her head. "Kinda strange that a fire would start in a building no one's been using for so long. That's the kind of fire that officials would want to investigate to ensure there was no foul play."

"Foul play?" I reply, my voice rising. "That's ridiculous. The barn was standing in the middle of barren fields and there was no hazard to anyone. I don't know what the big deal is."

"You know, I heard talk that you got that old barn fixed up last fall."

My throat tightens and I find it difficult to breathe. "Who told you that?"

"Cause if that barn was fixed up, then wouldn't you have made an insurance claim or something?"

"Folks talk. They ain't always correct."

"Then you don't mind if I look around? To satisfy my curiosity."

She's got me trapped. I could say no and ask if she's run this by Ferg. I could insist that she get a search warrant. But I don't want to give the appearance that I'm guilty of something. Like what's she going to find there? "You know, Ferg is aware of the fire. I told him at the time, and he said it was no big deal. But go right ahead. Like I've said, I'm pretty busy with things here."

"I won't be bothering you anymore. Thanks for your cooperation." With that she walks out of the greenhouse and drives off in her cruiser in the direction of the burned down barn.

I'm shaking as I pull out my phone. I struggle to stay calm enough to text Ferg.

That fucking Nadine has been nosing around and now is checking out the old barn site.

WTF!

You better do something and fast.

I'll be right there.

I pace out front of the greenhouse, waiting for Ferg to show up. Those are the longest fifteen minutes of my life. When he pulls up next to me, he rolls down the window. "Where is she?"

"She's still over at the old barn."

"Hop in."

I scramble into the passenger seat. "I fucked up some more."

"What do you mean?"

"I called that contractor to do a clean up of the fire scene, but he refused to do it."

"So, it's not been touched?"

"Nope."

"Jesus Murphy."

We race over the west end of the farm. Ferg parks next to Nadine's cruiser, and we get out, but she's nowhere in sight. Then I see her climb over the ridge behind where the barn sat. I nudge Ferg and point in Nadine's direction. "Fuck," I mumble under my breath.

We walk in Nadine's direction and meet her about halfway. "Stutz, what are you doing here?" barks Ferg. "Didn't I tell you not to be poking your nose around here? I never assigned you to investigate a fire."

"I know, I know. But it's a good thing I did," she sputters. It's obvious she's not about to back down. "This fire looks highly suspicious."

I glance over at Ferg, trying not to show any panic. "That's bullshit."

"What are you talking about?" replies Ferg. "Nadine, it was a barn fire."

"When a wood structure burns down, all that should remain is ash." She walks over to what's left of the barn. We follow right behind her. "Looks at this," she says, bending down. "This looks like the remnants of metal beams. And there's molten glass everywhere."

"Is there a point you're trying to make?" asks Ferg.

"I'm not done yet," responds Nadine. "Did the barn have electrical power?"

"No," I respond.

"Take a whiff of the air. Even two months later, it has the distinct odor of an electrical fire. So, what was going on here?"

"Enough already!" roars Ferg. "I want you to clear out of here."

"Sergeant, I know this is family," says Nadine, kicking at some the burnt remains. "I need you step back from this. Remember, you're also a cop."

"Nothing was going on here," I insist.

"And I got another question. I was walking around the perimeter and noticed in that gully behind here a freshly dug up area. If I were to dig that up, what would I find?"

I've had enough of Nadine and her questions. I've had enough of lying. I've had enough of this dirty business. I pull out my revolver from my waistband. "Get your fucking hands up." Nadine glares at me. "I said get them up!"

Nadine slowly raises her arms but says nothing.

"Think about what you're doing, Mac," says Ferg. His constant smirk is gone, and his face is like a ghost. "Put your gun down."

"I've had enough of this horseshit. I'm tired of being harassed by her. She's going to be joining those two drug dealers in that grave behind you."

Nadine doesn't look terribly shaken. It's as if she doesn't believe I would do it. She takes a step toward me. "There's no way you're going to get away with this. It's best if you give yourselves up."

"Just shut your trap! I want you to slowly take your gun out of the holster and toss it to me."

Nadine unsnaps her gun holster and pulls out her revolver holding it between her thumb and index finger. She slowly bends down and places it on the ground. She stands back up and kicks it toward me with a boot. When she is done, Nadine looks over at Ferg. "Are you going to stand there and watch him shoot me?"

"Come on Mac, you're putting me in a horrible position. Put the gun down, and let's talk this through."

"I'm done talking." I walk toward Nadine's gun and stoop down to scoop it up. Nadine charges forward as I'm hunched over and knocks me over. She jumps on top of me and grabs for the revolver in my hand. She is a lot stronger than I had ever imagined. I take a knee to the groin, and my grip on the revolver slips away. As

I grab hold of it again with my other hand, a shot goes off. A sharp pain spreads through my chest, and I release my grip on the gun.

I roll over onto my back, looking at the sky. I'm having trouble breathing. I put my hands on my chest, which slowly become covered with a feel a warm, sticky liquid. There are voices but I can't make out who they belong to. The summer breeze engulfs. I shut my eyes, and everything goes black.

THE END

ACKNOWLEDGEMENT

No book can be published with a group of people behind the scenes supporting the author. Thanks to Mica Kole and Melanie Lopata for your editing help; Rebecca Yelland for designing the cover and marketing material; Dave Loewith for graciously showing me around your dairy farm; Martine Oullette, Liz Poyser, Eden Boudreau, Karen Hubbard, Caytlyn Brooke, and Louise Rogers for providing feedback through the writing process. Most of all, thank you to my wife Mary Anne who has always been my biggest supporter.

ABOUT THE AUTHOR

Author Willie Handler was a satirist well before he became a novelist. Hailing from Canada, where self-deprecating humor is part of the national character, he finds targets for his humor everywhere. His targets include friends, family, co-workers, politicians, farmers, subway passengers, bureaucrats, telemarketers, Martians and his barber, Vince. His first book, *The Road Ahead*, is a biting political satire. Book two, *Loved Mars Hated The Food*, is a hilarious space adventure populated with aliens and bots. With his most recent work, he has crossed over to the world of black comedy.

Follow Willie on Twitter @WillieHandler for his humorous observations on life, marriage, and his obsession with coffee

NOTE FROM THE AUTHOR

Word-of-mouth is crucial for any author to succeed. If you enjoyed *Deep Into the Weeds*, please leave a review online—anywhere you are able. Even if it's just a sentence or two. It would make all the difference and would be very much appreciated.

Thanks!
Willie Handler

We hope you enjoyed reading this title from:

BLACK ROSE writing™

www.blackrosewriting.com

Subscribe to our mailing list – *The Rosevine* – and receive **FREE** books, daily deals, and stay current with news about upcoming releases and our hottest authors.
Scan the QR code below to sign up.

Already a subscriber? Please accept a sincere thank you for being a fan of Black Rose Writing authors.

View other Black Rose Writing titles at www.blackrosewriting.com/books and use promo code **PRINT** to receive a **20% discount** when purchasing.

CPSIA information can be obtained
at www.ICGtesting.com
Printed in the USA
BVHW070833150322
631199BV00004B/17

9 781684 339464